Little Red Riding Wolf

ORCHARD BOOKS
96 Leonard Street, London EC2A 4XD
Orchard Books Australia
14 Mars Road, Lane Cove, NSW 2066
First published in Great Britain in 1998
First published in paperback in 1999
Reprinted in 1998
Text © Laurence Anholt 1998
Illustrations © Arthur Robins 1998
The rights of Laurence Anholt to be identified as the author
and Arthur Robins as the illustrator of this work have been
asserted by them in accordance with the Copyright, Designs
and Patents Act, 1988.
A CIP catalogue record for this book is available
from the British Library.
1 86039 609 7 (hardback)
1 86039 649 6 (paperback)

Little Red Riding Wolf

Written by Laurence Anholt
Illustrated by Arthur Robins

These stories have not been tested on animals.

 ORCHARD BOOKS

In the very darkest corner of the deep dark wood sat the Big Bad Girl.

The Big Bad Girl was just about as
BIG and BAD as a girl can be, and all
the woodland animals were afraid of her.

She hung about beside the forest path and carved her name on trees. She shouted rude things at any little animal who passed by.

The Big Bad Girl tripped up little deer. She stole fir cones from baby squirrels and threw them at the poor little hedgehogs. The woodland birds didn't dare to sing when the Big Bad Girl was around!

But the person the Big Bad Girl liked to tease most of all was a charming little wolf cub who often passed by on his way to visit his dear old granny wolf.

Little Wolfie was the sweetest, fluffiest, politest little cub you could ever hope to meet. He would run along the path, *skippety-skip*, carrying a basket of freshly baked goodies for Old Granny Wolf, singing all the time…

"I'm a little wolfie, good and sweet
I am tidy, I am neat.
With a basket full of lovely grub,
I am Granny's favourite cub."

"Wot's in yer basket today, Little-Weedy-Wolfie-Wimp?" snarled the Big Bad Girl. "Mmmm, apple pies? I'll take those. Jam sandwiches? Very tasty."

"Oh dear, oh dear! Now there will be nothing for dear Old Granny Wolf," wailed Little Wolfie. And his little wolfie tears rolled into the empty basket.

Now, the Big Bad Girl's father was not big
and bad at all. He was a kind old hat-maker
who loved hats in every shape and size, and
thought everyone should wear one night
and day.

But the sad truth was, his hats were so awful that nobody would buy them. He had only sold one nightcap in his entire life, and the family was terribly poor.

"I can't understand it," he sighed. "I make these marvellous hats from dawn till dusk until my fingers are worn to the bone, but even my own daughter will not wear them. Please, my dear," he begged, "wear this one for me."

"Father," answered the appalling child, "I would rather wear one of your old socks on my head than this hat. Why can't you get a decent job? Nobody is a hatmaker these days. Couldn't you be a woodcutter like other people's dads?"

The Big Bad Girl hated hats so much that
as soon as her father gave her a new one, she
would run into the woods and give it to a
baby badger or a little squirrel to wear,
whether they liked it or not.

Then, to her father's dismay, she would return home, bare-headed, pretending she had lost the hat in the forest.

One day, however, the Big Bad Girl's father made her a hat that was more ridiculous than anything he had made before. This one was a real monster. It was bright red with a woolly bobble on top, little flaps over the ears and dangly bows to tie under the chin. It even had a small red cape to match. The old man was delighted with his creation. "Surely my daughter will LOVE this one," he laughed, jumping up and down with excitement.

But the Big Bad Girl said, "Father, you have made some vile things in your life, but this hat is THE PITS! I would rather wear your old underpants on my head. You have as much fashion sense as a dung-beetle!"

As her father lay weeping in his workshop, the Big Bad Girl stomped into the forest to find some unsuspecting little animal to wear the red riding hat.

But, alas, this one was so awful that no
one would touch it. Even the Woodland
Oxfam shop sent her away.

The Big Bad Girl sat by the forest path wondering what to do.

"Surely someone will be stupid enough to wear this hat," she said. As she spoke, she heard a delightful little song…

And who should come along the path,
skippety-skip, but Little Wolfie.

"Ah, ha!" sniggered the Big Bad Girl.
"Here comes Creepy-Cutesy-Custard-Cub.
My red riding hat would suit him perfectly!
I will trick him into wearing it. Then I will
make fun of him FOREVER! Heh heh
heh!"

"Where are you going, Little Fluffy Flea
Face?" growled the Big Bad Girl.

"I am off to visit my darling old granny wolf," replied Little Wolfie, politely.

"Well, I have just seen yer old granny wolf," lied the rotten girl. "You can't see her today because she is poorly and might give you her old granny wolf germs."

"Oh, poor old Granny Wolf," sighed Little Wolfie, sadly.

"But," continued the wicked girl, "she has made you a lovely sort of hat thing. She told me to give it to you and tell you never to take it off, night or day, even if people laugh at you."

Little Wolfie was very pleased…

…until he saw the revolting red riding hat.
Then even he had doubts.

But being a good little chap and wanting to please his granny, he tied it on his fluffy little head with the dangly ribbons.

The Big Bad Girl almost choked with laughter.

Holy Sweaty Snake Socks! she thought. This little wolf is UNBELIEVABLY stupid.

But Little Red Riding Wolf said 'thank you' politely and set off home, *skippety-skip*, chattering away to himself.

"How pleased I am with my new riding hat that Granny has made me. From now on I will call myself *Little Red Riding Wolf.* That will please her even more."

The Big Bad Girl rolled on the path and roared with laughter. "Holy Newt's Knickers! LITTLE RED RIDING WOLF!! What a name! A wolf should be called *Hairy Howler* or *Bone Cruncher* or *Old Yellow Eyes*. Little Red Riding Wolf is a TERRIBLE name."

All that day, Little Wolfie wore the red riding hat and tried not to notice when people laughed at him.

The next morning he said to himself, "Surely my dear old granny wolf will be better today. I will run along the path and show her how pleased I am with my lovely hat." And off he went, *skippety-skip*...

"I'm a little wolfie, so polite,
I am brave, I am bright,

I am happy, I am good,
In my new red riding hood."

BUT, by the side of the path, in the middle of the deep dark wood, blowing bubbles with her gum, something REALLY NASTY was waiting for him…

"I am not Tomato Head," said Little Red Riding Wolf, fighting back the tears. "I am Little Red Riding Wolf."

"Where are you going, Ketchup Cap?" demanded the Big Bad Girl, wiping her filthy nose on the back of her hand.

"I am going to dear Old Granny Wolf's house to see if she is better and to thank her for this lovely hat. Now, excuse me while I fill my basket with these pretty spring flowers for her kitchen table."

While Little Red Riding Wolf picked his flowers, the Big Bad Girl picked her nose thoughtfully. "That wrinkly Old Granny Wolf will spoil my fun," she said to herself. "I will take a shortcut to her house. If she gives me any trouble, I will lock her in the cupboard, then I will pretend that I am Old Granny Wolf. I bet she is even smaller and weedier than little Strawberry Top."

So the Big Bad Girl ran as quickly as she could to Old Granny Wolf's house. It was a very big house for a little old granny wolf.

But Granny Wolf was out chopping wood
in the forest.

The Big Bad Girl climbed in the back window and ran indoors, just as Little Red Riding Wolf tapped at the door.

"Old Granny Wolf, Old Granny Wolf. It is I, Little Red Riding Wolf, in my brand new hat."

"Holy Hopping Hedgehog Droppings!
That was quick," said the Big Bad Girl.
She ran up the stairs and searched for
somewhere to hide. She noticed a huge
bed, but how could she make herself look
like an old granny wolf?

On a hook on the
back of the door,
the Big Bad Girl
found Granny
Wolf's pink
lacy nightcap.
Little Wolfie
had bought it
for Granny
Wolf's
birthday, but
she never
really wore it.
Of course,
the Big Bad
Girl HATED
hats – and this
one was even
worse than the
red riding hat.

But the Big Bad Girl had no choice. She pulled the ghastly nightcap right down to her eyes and climbed into the bed, just as Little Red Riding Wolf came running up the stairs, *skippety-skip.*

"Granny Wolf, Granny Wolf. Where are you?" he called.

"Er, over 'ere, Little Woolly Hood Head," answered the Big Bad Girl.

"Oh Granny Wolf, Granny Wolf, thank you for the beautiful hat you made me. Doesn't it look wonderful?"

"Er…yeah, Little Bobble Brain…really wicked," replied the Big Bad Girl.

"But Granny Wolf, Granny Wolf, what a tiny voice you have and what small teeth you have too. Perhaps you are still poorly. You seem so pale and weedy today."

"Listen, Little Jam Man. You should learn not to make personal remarks!" snapped the Big Bad Girl.

"But Granny Wolf, Granny Wolf what small ears you have. In fact…I don't think you are my granny wolf at all. She is MUCH bigger than you."

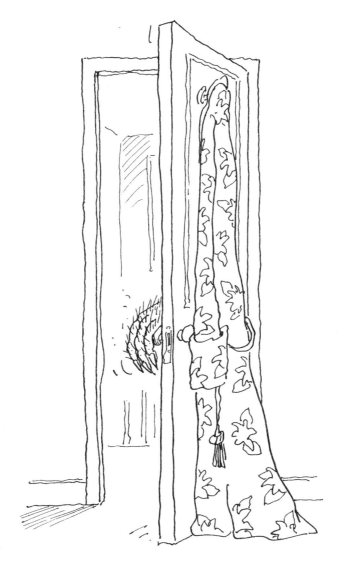

At that precise moment Granny Wolf
pushed open the door...

Granny Wolf was ENORMOUS.
She had huge yellow eyes,
big sharp teeth and
a long dribbly tongue.
She was carrying a
great sharp axe.

"Ah, Little Wolfie," she said. "What a nice surprise. You are just in time for tea. But why are you wearing that ridiculous hat? And what is this thing in my bed? It looks like a Big Bad Girl – a very tasty Big Bad Girl – just right for my BIG BAD TEA!"

The Big Bad Girl leapt out of bed, down
the stairs, out of the door, into the forest
and along the path as fast as her big bad legs
would carry her. She hammered on her
father's door.

"Father, Father," yelled the Big Bad Girl.
"Let me in. Let me in. I will be good. I will
do whatever you ask."

Her father peeped out of the window. He couldn't believe what he was seeing. There was his daughter wearing a delightful nightcap. It reminded him of one he had made himself many years before… He remembered it well because it was the only one he had ever sold.

"I will let you in," he said. "But only if you promise to wear a hat night and day – the one you are wearing now suits you beautifully!"

And so from that day on, the Big Bad Girl became a Big Good Girl (for most of the time). She found a job as a woodcutter, and her boss kept a very careful, big yellow eye on her.

The Big Good Girl kept her promise to wear a hat every day, although it was usually a chainsaw helmet.

And the red riding hat was useful…

...when they had an especially heavy load.

About the Autho

ephine Wilkinson is an author and historian. Sh
n the University of Newcastle where she also re.
is the author of *The Early Loves of Anne Bole*
raphy of Richard III, the first volume of whi
g King To Be, is published by Amberley. Sh
edition of Paul Friedmann's *Anne Boleyn*. Sh

by Josephine Wilkinson

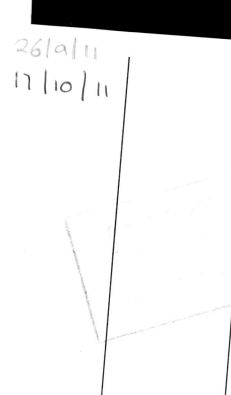

Mary Boleyn

Jose
from
She
biog
You
new

Also

Mary Boleyn

The True Story
of Henry VIII's
Favourite Mistress

JOSEPHINE WILKINSON

AMBERLEY

This edition first published 2010

Amberley Publishing Plc
Cirencester Road, Chalford,
Stroud, Gloucestershire, GL6 8PE

www.amberley-books.com

British Library Cataloguing in Publication Data.
A catalogue record for this book is available from the British Library.

ISBN 978 1 84868 525 3

Typesetting and Origination by Amberley Publishing.
Printed in Great Britain.

Contents

The Early Years, 1500–1514

In faith! welcome to me myself!

Both tradition and history associate the Boleyn family most closely with the beautiful castle of Hever, deep in the countryside of North Kent. It is here, it is often supposed, that the Boleyn children, Mary, Anne and George, were born.

Hever Castle was bought from Sir Thomas Cobham by Mary's great-grandfather, Sir Geoffrey Boleyn, who passed it on to his son, Sir William Boleyn of Blickling. Despite being called a castle, Hever[1] is in fact a comfortable, fortified manor house within curtain walls and surrounded by a moat. It features turrets and a small, cobbled courtyard enclosed by timbered buildings. It is entered through a gateway protected by a drawbridge, three portcullises and two pairs of doors. Between the doors, porters' lodges and 'murder holes' added further protection. Gunports in the upper facing of the side walls were rendered obsolete by the addition of windows by Sir William Boleyn. Sir William was still alive at the time of Mary's birth, so Hever did not descend to his eldest son, Mary's father, until 1505.

While it is possible that Mary Boleyn was born at Hever Castle, it is more probable that she came into the world at

Blickling Hall, near Aylsham in Norfolk. Blickling had been associated with royalty since its earliest days. It was once the property of Harold Godwinson, the last Saxon King of England and adversary of William the Conqueror. It is in keeping with its grand origins, then, that it should have strong connections with the Boleyn family, from the heart of which would spring a royal mistress, a gallant-about-court and a future Queen of England.

The present house dates as recently as the late seventeenth century, a superb example of Jacobean architecture. Previously, however, a fine manor house, built by Sir Nicholas Dagworth in 1401, stood on the site. The house owned by Harold Godwinson had either been replaced or extensively renovated.

Blickling Hall was acquired in 1616 by Sir Henry Hobart, who had enjoyed a lucrative career in law during the reign of Elizabeth I and was, at the time of his purchase, Lord Justice of the Common Pleas. Sir Henry had acquired Blickling from the Clere family, the heirs of Sir James Boleyn, Mary's uncle, who died in 1561. It was not long before Sir Henry embarked on a renovation programme of his own. His ambitions, however, overreached his purse and he was forced to retain much of the fabric of the old house within the new.

This happy turn of events allows us to take a glimpse of Blickling, as far as possible, as Mary would have known it. The house lies north to south, with the main entrance, reached by a little drawbridge, being on the south side. Within is a small court behind which lies the hall. This in turn opens out into the long court at the far side. On the east side is a parlour, a chapel and yonery, or vestry. Beyond the chapel and yonery are three lodgings. On the west side are the kitchen, the dairy and other such domestic spaces. The main staircase, which lies between the parlour and the chapel on the east side of the house, leads to the upper part of the main hall. To the left is a withdrawing chamber, which overlooks the entrance on the south side. To the right is a long gallery, which looks out onto the moat on the east side of the house and which leads to a side chamber from which the goings-on in the long court can be viewed. Nothing remains of the extensive gardens and woods; even those planted by Sir Henry Hobart have undergone much alteration.

The date of Mary's birth is as difficult to pinpoint as the place. No documents in which the event might have been recorded have survived, and such evidence that does exist is little more than circumstantial. To add to the difficulties it is not even clear in which order the Boleyn children were born. While the consensus seems to be that George, the only surviving son, was the youngest Boleyn, born in about 1504, historians have long argued about whether Mary or Anne was the elder.

Evidence of Anne's position as the eldest daughter comes from *A catalogue and succession of the kings, princes, dukes, marquesses, earles, and viscounts of this realme of England*, published in 1619 by Ralph Brooke, York Herald. Brooke refers to 'Anne, eldest daughter and co-heyre of Thomas Bullen'.[2] Adding that 'Anne the eldest, was first created Marchionesse of Penbroke [*sic*], & after married to King Henry the eight.

Mary the second daughter, married to William Carey, Esquire for the body to King Henry the eight.'[3]

In support of this is Weever's *Ancient Funerall Monuments*, published in 1631, which speaks of Anne's grave at St Peter ad Vincula: '[W]ithin the Quire of this Chappell, lieth buried the body of Anne Bullein, Marchionesse of Penbroke [*sic*], eldest daughter and coheir of Thomas Bollein...'[4] Weever also states that Anne was twenty-two years old when she returned to England and entered the service of Queen Katherine.[5] Since she returned to England at the end of 1521, this would give her a birth date of 1499.

Perhaps most compelling is the testimony of John Smyth of Nibley, who was a personal attendant, from 1584, of Thomas, the son and heir of Henry, Lord Berkeley. Lady Berkeley was the daughter of George Carey, second Lord Hunsdon, and so Mary Boleyn's great-granddaughter. In his *Lives of the Berkeleys*,[6] which he completed in 1618, Smyth states that William Carey 'maryed Mary second daughter and coheire of Thomas Bullein'.

That Mary was the second daughter and Anne the eldest would appear to be confirmed by evidence found on the tombstone of Lady Berkeley, who died in 1635. This states that her grandfather, Henry Carey, was the son and heir of William Carey and the Lady Mary Boleyn, his wife, second daughter and coheir of Thomas Boleyn, Earl of Ormond and Wiltshire.[7]

Such proof as that found on a tombstone must be considered persuasive, especially when it is seen in conjunction with supporting documents. It will be noticed, however, that each piece of evidence presented here is comparatively late.

In attempting to determine the relative ages of the Boleyn daughters, circumstantial evidence exists to suggest that Mary was, in fact, older than Anne.[8] Since both Mary and Anne had gone to France in 1514–1515, the dating of this appointment is not conclusive. That Anne remained in France for further training while Mary was brought back to England is certainly significant. Moreover, as shall be seen, Mary was sexually active while in France and she was launched at court before Anne. Mary was married in 1520, while plans for Anne's marriage were only seriously entered into the following year. Against this, it has been asserted, although without supporting evidence, that the Boleyns chose to break with the tradition of marrying their daughters in order of seniority.[9]

To solve the dilemma, the most obvious step is to return to the original sources, the earlier the better. One of the earliest contemporary sources is Anne's patent of creation as Marquis of Pembroke. This refers to her as 'Anne Rocheford, one of the daughters and heirs of Thomas earl of Wiltshire and Ormond'.[10] It might be suggested that, had she been the eldest, the patent would have said so.

A second and very important testimony concerns a letter written by Mary Boleyn's grandson, George Carey, the second Baron Hunsdon, to Lord Burghley. George Carey, it will be remembered, was the father of Lady Berkeley. In this letter, dated 6 October 1597, he asks advice about petitioning

Queen Elizabeth about his claim to the earldom of Ormond. This had been held by his great-grandfather, Sir Thomas Boleyn, who then lost it to his Irish cousin, Piers Butler.

The earldom of Ormond passed through the general line rather than being limited to heirs male. Hunsdon's claim was, therefore, based upon the assumption that the earldom should have passed to his father and then on to himself by virtue of their descent from Sir Thomas Boleyn's eldest daughter, Mary. In addition, he pointed out that there was no co-heir because the lands and title had gone to Hunsdon's grandmother as the sole heir, while her son, the first Baron Hunsdon, had sold the lands.

The earldom, therefore, consisted of a title only, to which Queen Elizabeth had no claim because she was the 'daughter and heir of Anne, youngest daughter of the said Sir Thomas Bullen, late earl of Ormond'. Hunsdon reiterated that, since his grandmother was the eldest daughter, the earldom ought to descend to him.[11]

In fact, at the time Baron Hunsdon was contemplating making his claim, the earldom of Ormond apparently rested with Thomas Butler, the grandson of Piers Butler. However, Baron Hunsdon states that he had tried to find the Act of Parliament which would have proved that the Butlers had been awarded the title but had been unsuccessful. As such, the title rightfully belonged to Hunsdon's grandmother, Mary Boleyn, the elder daughter and sole heir to Sir Thomas Boleyn, Earl of Wiltshire and Ormond. It was on this basis that he made his claim.

Such evidence is compelling. Had he been mistaken, and

had he actually approached the Queen with the matter, Elizabeth could easily have corrected him and claimed the earldom for herself to dispose of as she pleased.

It can be accepted, therefore, that Mary was the eldest daughter of the Boleyns. Scholarly consensus generally holds that she was born *c.*1500 with Anne following a year or so later. Their father would later bemoan that, during the early years of his marriage, his wife brought him 'every year a child'.[12] Among these, in addition to Mary, Anne and George, were two other sons, Henry and Thomas, neither of whom survived infancy.

The Boleyn children enjoyed a conventional education. Mary and Anne acquired those accomplishments deemed essential for young ladies of their status. These were the essentials of reading and writing, sewing, embroidery, singing and dancing. They learned to play instruments such as the virginal and the lute. Outdoor pursuits were not neglected; Mary and Anne would learn to ride in the parklands surrounding the house, as well as archery and hunting. Most importantly, they would learn to obey the men in their lives; this meant, first of all their father, and then, once they were married, their husbands.

Table manners were naturally very important, especially in a woman. Also necessary was to learn to put God first. Children as well as adults were expected to rise early to say their prayers. The Boleyn children would not have neglected this sacred duty for the Boleyns were a family of firm religious beliefs.

Mary Boleyn lived at a time when the education of

daughters, while still an advanced concept, was gradually gaining acceptance. By far the greatest advocate of this was Sir Thomas More, who regarded women as no less intellectually capable than men. His own daughters, particularly his beloved Margaret, enjoyed an education that was far in advance of that received by the sons of some families. Thomas Boleyn also felt that his daughters should not be held back academically simply because of their sex.

As a boy, George Boleyn's education would have been more formal than that of his sisters. Tradition insists that he had been 'educated among the Oxonians', although no firm evidence supports this.

Another important lesson for Mary and Anne was a study of the history of their family. Its origins can be traced back to Salle in Norfolk, where Boleyns, or Bullens, had lived since at least 1318. Their rise to prominence took the classic path that was often carved out by a younger son. Geoffrey Boleyn (1406–1463) was the cadet of a Salle tenant farmer who had gone to London to make his fortune. He became a mercer, served as an alderman and crowned his success by being elected Lord Mayor of London for the year 1457–1458. Perhaps Geoffrey's greatest achievement, however, was to marry Lady Ann Hoo, daughter and co-heiress of Thomas Lord Hoo, a member of the Bedfordshire aristocracy. Geoffrey acquired Blickling Hall in Norfolk from Sir John Fastolf and the manor and castle of Hever in Kent from Sir Thomas Cobham.

Sir Geoffrey and Lady Anne had one son, William, born in

1451. William was created a Knight of the Bath by Richard III, although this did not prevent him serving Henry VII upon his accession in 1485. Sir William is listed among those charged with placing and guarding the beacons used to warn the people of the approach of the King's enemies.[13] Similarly, he was given a commission of array against the expected invasion by King Charles of France,[14] and, like his father before him, he climbed the social ladder by means of a prestigious marriage. Sir William's wife was Lady Margaret Butler, daughter and co-heiress of Thomas Butler, seventh Earl of Ormond. William and Margaret had ten children, most of whom would survive into adulthood. Their second child and eldest son was Thomas, the father of Mary Boleyn.

Thomas Boleyn was born in 1477, making him fourteen years older than Henry VIII. Like his father, he would also serve King Henry VII, such as in 1497 when they took up arms to help Henry defeat the Cornish rebels at Blackheath. When the time came for him to marry, he followed in the footsteps of his father and grandfather and took a bride from the aristocracy. The precise date at which Thomas married is unknown but it is widely believed to have been *c.*1498. His bride was Elizabeth, the eldest daughter of Thomas Howard, Earl of Surrey and future second Duke of Norfolk.

The Howards, like the Boleyns, had supported the Yorkist faction during the Wars of the Roses. Thomas Howard's father, Sir John, was created Duke of Norfolk by Richard III, while Thomas was created Earl of Surrey. Norfolk acted as steward at Richard's coronation, carrying the sword of state.

Both Norfolk and Surrey supported Richard during the Buckingham Rebellion in the autumn of 1483. At Bosworth, father and son fought on Richard's side. Norfolk was killed fighting for Richard, while Surrey was wounded and taken prisoner.

Surrey was attainted, stripped of his lands and titles and sent to the Tower where he was to remain for the next three years. During the rebellion by the Earl of Lincoln, Surrey was offered the chance to escape his prison, but he refused. Having had time to reflect on the past, he probably now understood that the only way he would regain his freedom, his titles and property and his family's prestige, would be to show loyalty to the new King, Henry VII. If so, his patience and common sense were rewarded. In 1489 he was restored as Earl of Surrey and his lands were returned to him. Surrey now served King Henry with as much loyalty as he had King Richard.

The Howards and the Boleyns might not have been social equals, but they were on a par in another way; a shared history linked the two families. This was most conspicuously exemplified by their loyalty to a fallen King and their ability to survive politically fraught times. It was no surprise, then, that Thomas Boleyn and Elizabeth Howard should marry. Still, it was yet another prestigious marriage for the Boleyns. For Thomas, an alliance with Elizabeth Howard brought more than manors and lands; it opened the door for him to enter royal service.

Thomas Boleyn's debut at court was marked by his presence at the marriage of Arthur, Prince of Wales and Katherine of Aragon in November 1501. Two years later he was chosen as a member of the escort taking Henry VII's daughter, Margaret, to Scotland for her marriage to King James IV.

It was upon the death of his father, Sir William Boleyn, in 1505, that Thomas moved his family away from Blickling Hall, which had been left to his younger brother, James. Instead, the family made Hever Castle their principal seat, and it is with Hever that the Boleyns would remain most closely associated.

Another death brought about more significant changes. In May 1509, Thomas Boleyn became squire of the body at the funeral of Henry VII. He was made Knight of the Bath at the coronation of Henry VIII the following month. From now on, Boleyn's court career was firmly established. Henry VIII made him keeper of the Exchange at Calais and of the Foreign Exchange in England in July 1509.

Sir Thomas Boleyn was dedicated to the service of himself and his King in equal measure. His political ambition aside, he was a cultured man, known for his piety and study of the scriptures, very able and highly talented. Among his talents was a flair for languages; he could speak Latin and was fluent in French. Another was his superb ability as a sportsman. Boleyn was an expert hawk handler, and he was equally confident with horses. One of his favourite games was bowls, but he especially loved to joust, a sport at which he excelled. In 1510, he faced Henry VIII himself in the lists. He jousted again the following year at the great Westminster challenge as one of the answers at a tournament held in honour of Queen Katherine, who had just given the King his longed-for heir, Prince Henry.

As always, jousts were a riot of colour, noise and excitement, a carry-over from the great days of chivalry. Sir Thomas and the Marquis of Dorset rode into the list together dressed as pilgrims of Saint James. They wore tabards of black velvet with palmer's hats on their helmets and carried long Jacob staves. Their horses were trapped with black velvet, and all these, tabards, hats and traps, were set off with scallop shells of fine gold and stripes of black velvet each set with a golden scallop shell. Even their servants wore black satin with scallops of gold on the breast. Tragically, not long after this happy and exhilarating event, Sir Thomas was called upon to act as a bearer at the funeral of the young prince, who died after only fifty-two days of life.

Later in 1511, Boleyn was created joint Constable of Norfolk Castle and Sheriff of Kent with his neighbour, Sir Henry Wyatt, the father of the famous poet, Thomas Wyatt. In fact, the romantic Thomas Wyatt would become firm friends, or perhaps more than that, with the younger Boleyn daughter, Anne.

It was Boleyn's skill as a linguist, specifically his fluency in French, that marked him out as the best man to act as ambassador to the Low Countries. He set out with John Young and Sir Richard Wingfield to meet the Emperor Maximilian in 1512. The three men, joined by Sir Edward Poynings, concluded a treaty with the Pope and Margaret of Austria at Mechelen for a Holy League against France. This embassy would last for just over a year by which time Boleyn was in a position to join the invasion of France with a retinue of 100 men.

It was at about this time, according to the Victorian historian Agnes Strickland, that Mary's mother, Elizabeth, died of puerperal fever and that her father married a Norfolk woman of humble origin.[15] Similarly, the antiquary, Thoms,[16] asserts that Queen Elizabeth had 'numerous maternal relations and many of them among the inferior gentry (particularly in Norfolk)'. This was due, according to Thoms, to Sir Thomas Boleyn having selected a woman of lowly status as his second wife; a woman chosen, moreover, 'whilst the blood of the Boleynes was widely diffused with intermarriages of numerous junior branches'. As a result of this, according to Thoms, Queen Elizabeth was keen to suppress such claims of kindred. She was so sparing in her honours that her cousin-german, Lord Hunsdon, was never advanced above the rank of baron. Lord Hunsdon's brother-in-law, Francis Knollys, was not even made a peer, but only a Knight of the Garter. Greater honours would not come to the family until the reign of King Charles I. This tradition, however, finds no support. There is simply no evidence to suggest that Elizabeth Howard died as early as 1512.

Thomas Boleyn's mission to the Low Countries brought him into contact with Archduchess Margaret of Austria, the daughter of Emperor Maximilian. Margaret had been married three times in rapid succession. Her first husband, for whom she left her home to live in France at the age of three, repudiated her in favour of Anne of Brittany. Next, Margaret married Juan of Aragon, the brother of Queen Katherine. Juan died prematurely, leaving Margaret a widow at the age of seventeen. Four years later she married Philibert II, Duke of Savoy, who died in 1504. At only twenty-four years of age, Margaret returned to her native Netherlands to act as regent for her nephew, the future Emperor Charles V.

Margaret was a woman of refined tastes and excellent learning. She supervised the education of Charles and his sisters, Eleanor, Elizabeth and Mary. However, despite her three marriages, Margaret had no children of her own; her one recorded pregnancy resulted in a stillbirth. She was able to converse in French and Latin, and was an accomplished poetess in both languages. She was also a skilful politician.

These qualities struck a chord with Thomas Boleyn who, of course, shared many of them. Moreover, both their families had been supporters of the defeated Yorkist regime. Margaret was named after Margaret of York, the sister of Edward IV and Richard III, who became the third wife of Charles the Bold, Duke of Burgundy, the archduchess's grandfather. Margaret of York had been active in several conspiracies against the new Tudor regime. The archduchess had continued her family's support of, and affection for, the English, especially those associated with the Yorkists, such as Thomas Boleyn.

Despite her formidable character – she was formally styled *Très Redoutée Dame*, 'Most Dread Lady' – Sir Thomas felt perfectly at ease in the archduchess's presence. A charming anecdote tells of his being invited by Margaret to lay a wager concerning the conclusion of the ongoing negotiations. Sir Thomas was more than pleased to take her up on it. The archduchess staked a Spanish courser, while Sir Thomas promised to give her a hobby should she win.[17] As it turned out, Sir Thomas found himself in proud possession of the courser.

Thomas Boleyn's easy relationship with Margaret gave him the confidence to approach her about a matter of some importance concerning his family. While his daughters had received an education suited to their sex and social standing, it would be of immense benefit if they could be placed into households where they might be 'finished'; a place where they could learn courtly ways and achieve a polish that could not be acquired elsewhere. With this in view, Sir Thomas asked Margaret if she would consider taking one of his daughters as a young ward. Margaret, in her turn, entertained this request with due seriousness. To Thomas's delight, she agreed willingly.

It was now Sir Thomas's task to decide which of his daughters he should place with the archduchess. Mary was the appropriate age for a maid of honour, according to Emperor Maximilian's calculation,[18] that is to say, between thirteen and fourteen years of age. Tradition or etiquette might perhaps dictate that, as the eldest, she should be the one chosen. For Sir Thomas, this was not necessarily to be the deciding factor. It was a marvellous opportunity for advancement that must not be wasted. Clearly, the sister who would most benefit from such a placing should be the one to go.

Mary Boleyn has been described as 'a placid, unremarkable girl',[19] of a 'giddy' disposition, unlike her 'far more intelligent and far more applied' sister, Anne.[20] Perhaps this is also how Thomas Boleyn saw his daughters when he compared them. If so, perhaps he did not expect Mary to shine. We cannot know whether she excelled in the languages that were so easily mastered by her father and brother, and for which her sister was to become so famous. No one bothered to record her abilities in this area.

Conversely, it could be argued that Mary's grasp of French was actually better than her sister's. As such, Anne should be the one to go to the Archduchess Margaret, whose court would provide a better environment for her to learn a language that had so far eluded her. It is also possible that, as the elder sister, Mary's education was more complete than Anne's and she was less in need of such an opportunity. Whatever the case, it was Anne Boleyn, at the age of twelve or so, who crossed the Channel to the court of Archduchess Margaret of Austria in the early summer of 1513, while Mary remained in England.

That one of the reasons Anne Boleyn had gone to the court of the archduchess was in order to learn French is confirmed by the letter she sent to her father. In the letter, which was written in French, Anne apologises for her spelling. She then assures her father that, knowing that the queen will wish to speak to her, she will persevere in learning to speak French well.

However, just over a year later, events conspired that would ensure that Anne would not remain at the archduchess's court for very much longer. The time was fast approaching when the Boleyn sisters would be reunited.

CHAPTER 2

Mary in France, 1514–1520

I am as I am, and so I will be;

But how that I am, none knoweth truly.

Early in the year 1514, King Henry's younger sister, the most beautiful and delicate of all the Tudor roses, Princess Mary, was preparing for marriage. Like many princesses, her journey towards this event had been long and somewhat winding. When she was only two and a half years old, the Duke of Milan, Ludovico Sforza, put forward his son, Massimiliano, as a suitor. Massimiliano was about the same age as the princess but, although the offer of his hand was sincere, it was rejected by Mary's father, Henry VII. Then, when Mary was ten, a chance visit to the court by Philip the Handsome, the King of Castile, opened the way for her betrothal to his grandson, Charles of Ghent, the future Emperor Charles V. The betrothal was formalised at Richmond in 1508, when Princess Mary was thirteen years old. Upon the death of her father, the princess officially became known as Archduchess of Burgundy and Princess of Castile.

The prospect of his sister's marriage to Charles delighted Henry VIII, who needed support in his quest to re-establish an English presence in France. Henry's marriage to Katherine of Aragon shortly after his accession was partly to do with securing her father, King Ferdinand, as an ally. The wedding of Princess Mary and Charles would bring him another.

The marriage was expected to take place in May 1514, when Charles turned fourteen. As things turned out, Ferdinand of Aragon turned his back on an English alliance and made peace with France instead. Even worse, Emperor Maximilian also began to show a reluctance to allow the marriage to go ahead. He, too, was negotiating a secret pact with France behind Henry's back, the outcome of which was a separate peace. He was also searching for a new bride for his son, Charles. King Henry was furious. Acting on the advice of Thomas Wolsey, he instructed Mary to repudiate her marriage contract with Charles. Meanwhile, a new peace treaty between England and France was sealed by Mary's betrothal to the French King, Louis XII.

King Louis XII of France was not the most desirable marriage partner for any woman, especially not for a woman as young, beautiful and passionate as Princess Mary. She was a vigorous nineteen years of age; he was fifty-two and aged even by the standards of the day. He suffered from various infirmities, most obviously gout, and was not expected to live much longer. At first the princess refused to countenance such a proposition, but her love for her brother and her sense of duty ensured that any protest must be short-lived. She was married by proxy on 18 August, with the Duc de Longueville standing in for Louis. This event was a significant one in the life of Princess Mary, or the French Queen as she was now to be known. It was to be even more so for the Boleyn daughters, Mary and Anne, for the princess had requested them to accompany her to France and to attend her in her new life.

At the age of fourteen, Mary was just the right age to make her debut as a maid of honour. Arrangements were easily made for her. While Anne had gone over to the court of the Archduchess Margaret to further her education, Mary remained in England. She might have stayed at the family home at Hever Castle, but it is equally possible that she had been placed in the household of some notable, a friend of her father's, perhaps, to give her a final 'polish'. Unfortunately, Mary's whereabouts and her activities at this time are a mystery; anything said at this point could only be conjecture.

Mary's father, however, was busily making arrangements for Anne. Since she, too, was to join the French Queen as one of her attendants, it was necessary to persuade Archduchess Margaret to release her. In this, Sir Thomas had to muster all his powers of diplomacy because Margaret was very unhappy about the betrothal of the French Queen and Louis XII. Margaret had wanted the princess, to whom she still referred to as the Princess of Castile, as a bride for her nephew, and was not at all pleased when the plan had fallen through. Despite the fact that the betrothal had been publicly repudiated by the princess, Margaret refused to accept it; nor would she acknowledge the new alliance between the princess and King Louis. Eventually, however, she saw reason and allowed herself, reluctantly, to be persuaded to allow Anne to leave.

The French Queen, accompanied by a magnificent entourage, prepared to leave England for her new life at the French court. As the first stage of her journey she travelled to Dover with King Henry and Queen Katherine and the rest of the court amid turbulent winds and foul weather. On 2 October, at about four in the morning, the weather calmed sufficiently to allow the ships to leave. The young French Queen bade a tearful farewell to Katherine and, accompanied by her brother, hurried to the water's edge to embark.

It is possible that Anne Boleyn reached Dover in time to accompany her new mistress to France, but her name does not appear on the lists. Only one Boleyn is noted to have taken the ship with the French Queen: Mary, who is listed as 'M. Boleyne'.[1]

The fleet that was to take the French Queen to France consisted of fourteen vessels of the English navy, several of them carrying her wardrobe, her treasure, horses and the baggage of her ladies and companions. Barely had the fleet completed a quarter of its journey when a huge storm blew up and scattered the ships in all directions. It was certainly a rough crossing, with some ships making land at Calais, others at various ports in

Flanders, while one, the *Lubeck*, came to grief on the coast of France near Calais with the loss of several hundred hands.

The ship carrying the French Queen maintained its course towards Boulogne. However, the pilot, unable to steer into the harbour entrance, was forced to ram the ship ashore. Sir Christopher Garnish, standing in the breakers awaiting his mistress, gallantly took her up in his arms and carried her ashore.[2] Such was the entrance to her new kingdom as made by the fair Queen of France. History does not record how her maids coped, but it can be guessed that they were just as seasick and as much in need of chivalrous assistance as their mistress.

Having survived the turbulence of a Channel crossing in autumn, the French Queen began her journey towards Abbeville, where she was to make her formal entrance into France. According to custom, King Louis did not come to meet her; but, so anxious was he to see his new bride, he 'accidentally' encountered her train while he was out hunting.

On setting eyes upon his Tudor rose, the old King's heart leapt. Indeed, he had cause to be excited. She was petite, poised and beautiful, with red-gold hair and the pale translucent complexion that usually accompanies it. She was the ideal picture of womanhood, certainly, and the quintessence of Tudor beauty.

Louis' delight in his new bride was diminished somewhat when he saw the size and the composition of her entourage. Consisting of more than one hundred people, he felt it was too large; even worse was the fact that they were all English. An unhappy experience with his first wife's Breton attendants had persuaded him that his Queen should be attended by French ladies, whom he could trust to place French interests above all others. His sentiments were probably also influenced by the recent war between his country and England and the residual hostility that existed between the common people of both countries. Under the circumstance, Louis thought it a prudent move to dismiss all but a handful of the Queen's English retinue. Still, among those allowed to remain in France was 'Madamoyselle Boleyne'.[3]

The French Queen was quite indignant at this weeding out of her attendants, not least because it deprived her of the matriarchal Lady Jane Guildford. This loss was the more keenly felt because Lady Jane had acted as an unofficial surrogate mother to the princess following the death of her mother, Elizabeth of York, when the princess was only fourteen years old. The removal of Lady Jane left the French Queen feeling alone and vulnerable.

It was true that those who survived the pruning were closer to her own age, but this was not necessarily a good thing. The French Queen worried about what might become of her should she fall ill. What she meant was: who would look after her if she became pregnant? As she saw it, she was left with women and maidens 'such as never had experience nor knowledge how to advertise or give me counsel in any time of need'.[4] Certainly, at the age of only fourteen, the unmarried Mary Boleyn was still inexperienced in such matters, as were her companions.

In desperation the French Queen wrote to her brother and also to Wolsey, begging them to intervene on her behalf. However, they were reluctant to interfere with King Louis' domestic arrangements, and so the new Queen settled down to married life as best she could. Her personal feelings notwithstanding, she had the good sense to accept what had happened and to make the best of it. There was, after all, the hope that Louis might not live very long and she would soon be free to lose herself in a relationship with a man she really wanted.

In fact, life at the French court did have its pleasures. Louis usually spent his winters at his château at Blois in the stunning Loire valley. However, grief for his first wife, who had died at the château the previous spring, kept him away and he spent the winter of 1514–1515 at Paris.

The court divided its time between several royal palaces in the city and the surrounding areas. One was the dark and imposing Louvre, with its magnificent gardens and its close proximity to the Seine. It had been extended and redecorated during the previous century by Charles V of France, but was now looking more than a little tired. Then there was the beautiful Château de Vincennes set in the country beyond the city walls to the east. It was here that the royal nursery had been installed, for which, it is safe to say, the Queen was expected to provide another resident. Still another was

Saint-Germain-en-Laye to the west of Paris where the court spent three weeks, a sort of honeymoon for the royal couple. Mary Boleyn's life as maid of honour to the Queen of France was one of gaiety, a seemingly endless round of dancing, singing and music, while the jousting was every bit as exciting to watch in France as it had been in England.

As Mary followed her mistress to each of these exciting palaces, her beauty ensured that she would never be short of suitors sighing after her. It was a heady time which Mary, free of her father's guiding influence for the first time, was determined to enjoy to the full.

Then, on 1 January 1515, Louis XII died. One tradition has it that he had been danced to death by his energetic young wife; another suggests that his death was attributable to his exertions in the bed chamber. The King was indeed uxorious and, despite his frailty, boasted of having 'crossed the river' three times on his wedding night. Whatever the case, the French Queen was now officially the White Queen. This change of title, which the Queen refused to adopt, came from the custom that French Queens wore white as a sign of mourning. While the Queen might have worn the traditional white, she did not mourn her late husband too deeply, for she intended to capitalise on her new-found freedom; and this she would do in a most spectacular way.

Nevertheless, the French Queen, in the early days of her widowhood, was vulnerable. Her position, as well as that of Mary Boleyn and the Queen's other attendants, was not one to be envied because they and their futures were now in the hands of the new King of France, François I. Following royal protocol, the White Queen had been sent away upon becoming a widow, in this case to the Hôtel de Cluny, for a period of 'quarantine' in case she was carrying the late King's baby. If so, that child, if a boy, would be the new King of France. As it was, François had not waited for confirmation or otherwise of the Queen's pregnancy. He took the throne straight away because a long minority and regency would have been undesirable considering the politically delicate situation France faced at the time.

King François was the son of Louise de Savoy, first cousin to the late King Louis. He was nineteen, the same age as the French Queen, and married to Claude of France, Duchess of Brittany. Queen Claude was the eldest daughter of King Louis by his beloved Anne of Brittany. Because of France's adherence to the Salic law, which barred women from inheriting a throne or fief, Louis was succeeded by his nearest male relative, his son-in-law, François.

François was similar to King Henry in many ways. They were both young, incredibly vain and eager to establish themselves as significant players on the political stage of Europe. Silvester de Giglis described François as 'tall and broad-shouldered, with an oval and handsome face, very slender in the legs, and much inclined to corpulence'.[5] An amusing account of a conversation between the Venetian diplomatist Pasqualigo and Henry VIII concerns the former's meeting with the new King of France. Henry walked over to where Pasqualigo was sitting and questioned him about François:

> 'The king of France, is he as tall as I am?' I told him there was but little difference. He continued, 'Is he as stout?' I said he was not; and then he enquired, 'What sort of legs has he?' I replied 'Spare', whereupon he opened the front of his doublet, and placing his hand on his thigh, said, 'Look here; and I have also a good calf to my leg'.[6]

The Kings competed in another area too, that of power. As things now stood, François had an advantage over Henry: he had Henry's sister as a 'guest' in his country and it was to his advantage to keep her there. Under the terms of her marriage contract with Louis XII, if the Queen decided to return to England upon becoming a widow, François would have to return her dowry and trousseau and pay her a large dower each year for as long as she lived. The French Queen would also be at liberty to take with her the gifts of jewellery and plate presented to her by the late King. These included a 'great diamond and a tablet with a great round pearl'.[7]

It was much better, from François' point of view, to marry her off to his own advantage. The courts of Europe were already expressing their interest. One strong candidate was the Duke of Lorraine. Another was the Duke of Savoy, but the Emperor Maximilian, the Duke of Bavaria and the Prince of Portugal all saw themselves as worthy suitors for the hand of the princess who, as far as those who chose to believe the rumours were concerned, was, in fact, still a virgin. The French Queen, with Mary Boleyn in tow, could end up anywhere.

Then again, the French Queen had ideas of her own in the matter of her remarriage. Just prior to leaving for France, she had struck a bargain with her brother. She would agree to marry King Louis, stating once again for good measure that it was the last thing she would do if given a choice. However, she would do so only on condition that her next marriage would be to a man of her own choosing. Now that fate had set her at liberty, she wrote to Henry reminding him of the bargain they had made.[8]

It is possible that the Queen already had a candidate in mind. It was no secret that she was attracted to Charles Brandon. A close friend to Henry, Brandon had recently been invested Duke of Suffolk, a title previously held by the Yorkist de la Pole family. Indeed, the French Queen had been infatuated with Suffolk from at least the time of her engagement to Charles, nephew of the Archduchess Margaret and, it seems, her affection had been returned.

Brandon was certainly an interesting character. Twelve years older than the French Queen, he had enjoyed a tumultuous marital life which saw him, at one stage, married to three women at the same time. His first wife was Anne Browne, a gentlewoman in the service of Queen Katherine. Upon their betrothal, the couple had consummated their union and Anne became pregnant. Although the consummation had made their betrothal legally binding, Suffolk abandoned her in order to marry her widowed aunt, Dame Margaret Mortimer, instead. Then, after just over a year of marriage to Dame Margaret, he sought to annul their union on the grounds of consanguinity. This stemmed from the fact the Dame Margaret's first husband and Brandon's grandmother were related; then there was the not-so-small matter of his still existent tie with Dame Margaret's niece, Anne, which brought with it the impediment of affinity. It was at about this time also that Suffolk fathered three illegitimate children. Even so, he went on to contract a new marriage, this time to Lady Lisle.

This, then, was how matters stood with the gallant Charles Brandon as he embarked for France in the entourage of the French Queen for whom the old adage about love being blind seemed to have been coined. Suffolk, who had just returned to England after discharging his duty, was sent back to France as soon as the news of the death of King Louis had arrived. He was detailed to congratulate the new King on his accession, to take advantage of King François's wish to recover Tournai and, last but not least, to gain possession of the jewels presented to the French Queen upon her marriage to the late King.

It was, perhaps, with a view to marrying Suffolk that the French Queen had extracted the promise from Henry that she would be allowed to choose her next husband. Cardinal Wolsey certainly appears to have thought so. He wrote to her during Louis XII's last illness to warn her against contracting a new marriage. She wrote back to say that she was not so childish as to do such a thing. Wolsey's warning, however, put her on her guard; she began to fear that some other plan was being made for her. Events would soon confirm her suspicions.

Upon the death of King Louis, his successor lost no time in taking advantage of the vulnerable widow. The sequence of events is difficult to piece together because, by their very nature, it was necessary to proceed as discreetly as possible.

According to the French Queen's own testimony, François had visited her in her chambers and expressed his love for her. He offered to put away his wife, Queen Claude, so that he could marry her. When the young widow refused his suit, he made improper advances towards her. The French Queen, more vulnerable than ever and deeply afraid, turned to the one person she thought would help her: the Duke of Suffolk.

For his part, King François's version of events differs somewhat from that of the Queen. He asserted that she had confided in him, confessing her love for Suffolk. She told him of her fears that her brother was planning another dynastic marriage for her. She asked François for his support as she sought to marry, at last, the man she had wanted all along. In matters of love, what Frenchman, whatever his station, could refuse such a plea?

François's story is corroborated by the testimony of the Duke of Suffolk himself. He wrote that, shortly after arriving in France he had spoken to François. It was all very cordial, and the conversation focused entirely upon business. However, later, Suffolk was summoned back into François' presence. The mood had changed. King François accused the duke of planning to marry the French Queen, a charge Suffolk denied. Still, Suffolk was put on his guard and was concerned enough to write to Wolsey to inform him of what had happened.

As letter after letter crossed the Channel, Suffolk said that the French Queen had told him she was terrified of being forced into a second, unwanted marriage. She would, she said, rather be torn to pieces than make another such match. She then wept so much that Suffolk's heart went out to her. There was only one thing to do:

> [T]he queen would never let me be in rest till I had granted her to be married; and so to be plain with you, I have married her heartily, and have lain with her, insomuch as far [as in] me lies that she be with child.[9]

Such was the whirlwind romance of the Duke of Suffolk and the ex-Queen of France. The duke was coerced by womanly tears into marrying without permission, a marriage that was technically an act of treason for which Suffolk should have lost his head. All the while, their antics were being watched by the new duchess's ladies. What lessons might Mary Boleyn have learned from her mistress? Perhaps she came to see that, in matters of matrimony, if nothing else, a woman could have her own way if she was brave enough and determined enough to fight for what she wanted. It was a lesson she learned well and one she would apply in later years to her own advantage.

As for François, he had lost his first power-battle with Henry VIII, but there was another battlefield in which he would more than equal his English rival: that of romance. François, like Henry, was a married man and, again like Henry, this did not prevent him from indulging his passion for women. In fact, for François, infidelity was to become a fine art. Even while he was still Duc d'Angoulême his reputation had been established. His licentiousness was almost legendary. While the Queen of the late Louis XII remained a guest in his country, François saw to it that her ladies would never be lonely. One lady in particular had caught his eye: Mary Boleyn.

Quite to what extent Mary could be considered François' mistress cannot be said for certain. François would later state that he knew Mary in France *per una grandissima ribalda et infame sopre tutte* – 'for a great prostitute and infamous above all others'.[10] Somewhat ungallantly, he referred to her as his English Mare, boasting of the amount of times he had 'ridden' her.[11]

On the other hand, Mary was not, and would never be, François' *maîtresse en titre*, his official mistress, the first of whom would be Françoise de Foix. The experiences of the two women could not be more different. Madame de Foix was a distant relative of King François. She was betrothed to Jean de Laval in 1506 and gave birth to their daughter two years later. In 1509 the couple were married and were making their life together at Châteaubriant when François called them to court in 1516. It was not long before Madame de Foix's beauty and sophistication brought her to the King's notice. François showered her with gifts and favours. Her family also found favour: her husband was given offices, while her elder brother was made governor of the duchy of Milan; other brothers secured positions of high command in François' army. Madame de Foix became the official mistress of the King in about 1518, and by the following year, her position was obvious to all.

Madame de Foix's experience was in marked contrast to that of Mary Boleyn, who appears to have been used simply as a sex object. Her youth, beauty and inexperience led her into a series of short-lived encounters as she was passed from the King, who quickly tired of her, to his favourites. Such behaviour was not unique to French Kings, of course. It had also been witnessed in England, where Edward IV had been a past-master at it, much to the chagrin of his many mistresses; his grandson, Henry VIII, would continue the tradition.

Mary's own thoughts on the matter are unrecorded. She might even have found the distraction and, especially, the attention, welcome. However, the difficult situation in which her mistress and the English ladies found themselves following the death of Louis XII would suggest otherwise.

It would take a few weeks, but Wolsey did manage to pacify Henry and his privy council, who were baying for Suffolk's blood, sufficiently to allow the Duke and Duchess of Suffolk to return to England where they could begin their married life together.

What became of Mary at this point is not clear. Some historians[12] have argued that she remained in France with her sister and that the two Boleyn daughters became maids of honour to Queen Claude. While this was certainly true of Anne, there is no evidence to support such a conclusion for Mary.

The consensus of scholarly opinion[13] asserts that Mary returned to England at the same time as the new Duchess of Suffolk, or shortly afterwards, and was never in the service of Queen Claude. It could be speculated that she joined her mother as a maid of honour to Queen Katherine of Aragon. Again, however, there is no direct evidence for this. Nevertheless, it is a reasonable assumption. Her father was a respected courtier and a favourite with the King; and her mother, Lady Elizabeth, is known to have been in the service of the Queen.

It has been suggested that Mary fell out of favour with her family over her behaviour in France, where she had offended the code of discretion that existed even there.[14] As a result, she was recalled to England in disgrace. If so, her chances of finding a position in Katherine's household would have been seriously diminished. If this were the case, her disgrace was short-lived, as future events will show.

CHAPTER 3

First Marriage, 'Lady Carey' 1520

The heart and service to you proffer'd

With right good will full honestly,

Refuse it not since it is offer'd,

But take it to you gentely.

While nothing definite is known of Mary Boleyn's whereabouts immediately after her return to England, there is no ambiguity as to where she was or what she was doing on 4 February 1520. On this day Mary Boleyn, at the age of twenty, was married.

The circumstances of Mary's marriage are, like much about her life, shrouded in mystery. It cannot even be said with certainty that her husband was carefully chosen for her in the time-honoured fashion of high-born families, accompanied by the usual haggling over her dowry and jointure. As far as the sources are concerned, Mary's marriage came out of the blue. The Victorian historian, Agnes Strickland, notes Mary's 'incorrigible predilection for making love-matches', implying that Mary, like her former mistress, the French Queen, had lost her heart and married her beloved with no regard to the consequences.[1] Bruce agrees, stating that Mary compounded her problems with her family by entering into a marriage, presumably for love.[2]

It is not impossible that Mary's marriage was indeed the outcome of a romance in which she lost both her heart and her good sense. However, the fact that King Henry himself was a guest at the wedding would seem to preclude this. Marriages among the nobility carried enormous political implications. Whatever their personal feelings on the subject, the young couple had little choice but to comply with the decisions made by their elders.

It is even possible that Henry had organised Mary's marriage himself. Certainly he had involved himself with such matters before and would do so again. Shortly after Mary was married, Henry was making enquiries regarding a possible match between her sister, Anne, and James Butler. Letters to that effect would begin to appear as early as September 1520.

The man selected for Mary was William Carey. Attractive and athletic, an unfinished portrait dated a few years after his marriage, shows a young man of soft, handsome features. He is well dressed, as befitting his station and, although he holds a book, this does not necessarily indicate any especial learning. Rather, his distracted expression, as though deep in reverie, suggests a man of poetic inclinations. Although the book is closed, he marks his place with his finger, suggesting he is musing on something he has just read. It is a charming portrait and it is easy to imagine that Mary would not be dissatisfied with this enchanting young man as her husband.

William Carey's date of birth is not known, although the received opinion suggests the year 1500, making him about the same age as Mary. He was the son of Thomas Carey of Chilton Foliat in Wiltshire and the grandson of Sir William Carey of Cockingham in Devon. Sir William had been a steadfast supporter of the Lancastrian side during the Wars of the Roses and he was among those who had been beheaded by the victorious Edward IV in the bloody aftermath of the battle of Tewkesbury in 1471.

Thomas Carey, who had stood as MP for Wallingford in 1491–1492, died at about the time of his son's birth, leaving a widow, Margaret Spencer. Margaret was the daughter and co-heiress of Sir Robert Spencer of Ashbury in Devon. Sir Robert was the son-in-law of Edmund Beaufort, the first Duke of Somerset, having married the duke's daughter and co-heiress, Eleanor. Margaret's sister, Katherine, was married to Henry Algernon Percy, fifth Earl of Northumberland. As such, William Carey was well-connected. He was also of royal blood, being descended from Edward III, and a distant cousin to Henry VIII.

The death of his father meant that Carey had been given in wardship. It is possible that his mother took him in, although there was no guarantee that she would want to keep her son at home. An alternative option would have been to send the boy to the home of some influential person, who would then have control of his person, marriage and property during his minority. It is not known who this person might have been. It is not impossible that the boy was brought up in Devon, where he had relatives.

William Carey's Devon connections brought him into the sphere of Henry Courtenay, second Earl of Devon. The earl's father, William Courtenay, had been disgraced for his part in the conspiracy surrounding Edmund de la Pole, the Yorkist pretender and cousin of Henry VII's Queen, Elizabeth of York. William Courtenay was eventually restored to royal favour but died shortly after his creation as Earl of Devon. Henry succeeded to his father's title and sought to achieve the reversal of his father's attainder. He then entered court life in 1514, having been selected by the French King, Louis XII, to attend the new French Queen. As such, he probably knew Mary Boleyn. By 1519, Courtenay had established himself as a member of Henry VIII's household. One young man who was often seen in his company was William Carey; in fact it is possible that Courtenay had introduced Carey to court.

By 1519 William Carey, too, had officially become a member of King Henry's household. Actively involved in court life, he was entitled to a livery at breakfast and was a regular feature in the lists or at the tennis court. His growing intimacy with his royal distant cousin can be traced in his activities at the gambling table, where he was successful at taking the King's money. Carey, like Courtenay, was an accomplished jouster. Perhaps it was his skill in this area that most endeared him to Henry, who would have had ample opportunity to witness the young man's skill for himself. One such occasion could have been when Carey took part in the celebrations for the wedding of his friend Courtenay to Gertrude Blount.

Gertrude Blount was Henry Courtenay's second wife, his first having died a short time previously at the age of only fourteen. She was a kinswoman of Elizabeth Blount, who had recently given birth to King Henry's illegitimate son, Henry Fitzroy. It was perhaps this event, and the general aura of delight that surrounded it, that led to the King's blessing upon the new Courtenay marriage.

As was happening with ever greater frequency at Henry's court, young men in William Carey's position were exercising their influence over the King to a degree that disturbed certain, more senior members of the King's council. These included Cardinal Wolsey, the Duke of Norfolk, the Earl of Worcester and Sir Thomas Boleyn.

The concerns of the elder courtiers were probably prompted by the behaviour of some of the King's young gentlemen, such as Sir Edward Neville and Sir Francis Bryan. They had recently returned from the court of France, where they had accompanied King François in his boisterous adventures. On more than one occasion they had dressed in disguise and ridden through the streets of Paris throwing eggs, stones and whatever other missiles came to hand at the unsuspecting people. Returning to England, they had continued this behaviour, exchanging the streets and the people of Paris for those of London. To them it was a fine joke; to the members of Henry's council, it was unacceptable conduct that had to be curbed. They offered their opinion to the King and were relieved to find that he agreed with their views. Perhaps Henry had come to realise that the young men's over-familiarity with him was reaching an inappropriate degree. Whatever the case, the result was a great purge in which many of the King's young minions were banished from court. William Carey, however, was one of those who survived. Whatever influence he exercised over the King had clearly remained within the bounds of propriety. Carey continued as a royal favourite and was set on course for a successful and rewarding career at court.

In spite of this, it has been suggested that the match between Mary Boleyn and William Carey was not a particularly good one from the bride's perspective.[3] William Carey was a younger son without prospect of land or fortune. He had to depend upon the usual royal gifts of keeperships, stewardships and the occasional grant of a manor with which to maintain himself. As such, Mary's less than exemplary behaviour while in France and the undesirable reputation it had earned her might have led the Boleyns to think that the only thing they could do with their wild daughter was to marry her off to a man of no substance. The alternative would be to shut her away in a convent, a common practice among the upper classes described by Milton as 'convenient stowage for their withered daughters'.[4]

However, it is possible to take another view. Carey had been present at the court since at least 1519 as we have seen. He was the King's distant cousin, a royal favourite and involved in court life. Sir Thomas Boleyn had perhaps seen an advantage in having Carey as a son-in-law, not least because of his connection with the Earl of Northumberland. In not too many years hence, Mary's sister, Anne, would become involved with the earl's son and heir, Henry Percy. Although negotiations were underway for a marriage between Anne and James Butler, her father's attitude suggests that he might have preferred an alliance with the Percys. Also, Carey could prove a helpful ally in the Boleyns' power struggle with Cardinal Wolsey. The cardinal jealously guarded his own influence with the King and looked upon men such as Sir Thomas Boleyn and his Howard in-laws as a threat.

For Carey, an alliance with the Boleyns brought him into contact with some of the finest families in the land: the Bohuns, the Butlers and the Howards. Moreover, since Sir Thomas was an important courtier and a skilful politician, both the Boleyns and William Carey would benefit from the match.

Mary would have expected to have had little, if any, say in the selection of her husband.[5] There were sound and practical reasons behind this tradition, the origins of which were lost in the mists of time. There had long been dislike, even a suspicion, of passionate love between the sexes. Possibly this was connected to the fear that such love would lead to sin, the very sin for which, as St Paul notes, marriage was the only cure.

In addition to this, children were understood to be subject to parental control. This was natural in a society in which family discipline was seen as the best way to maintain public order and in a class in which men were not expected to work for a living. Sons were reliant upon their fathers for their income in the form of allowances. Daughters were especially dependent and protected. Regarded as the inferior sex, their obedience was usually guaranteed by the fact that even an unwanted husband was a better prospect than life as a spinster.

As the couple stood at the door of the church in Greenwich in the presence of God and exchanged their vows, we can only guess at which members of Mary's family attended. Her father certainly was not present, since he had been sent on a diplomatic mission to France and was not due to return for a few weeks. Mary promised to take William:

> to my wedded husband, to have and to hold from this day for better, for worse, for richer, for poorer, in sickness and in health, to be bonny and buxom, in bed and at board, till death us depart, if holy church will it ordain: and thereto I plight thee my troth.

Here, buxom meant compliant, lively and good-tempered, qualities which William would certainly wish for in his wife as he took the ring in his right hand. Placing it on Mary's left thumb, he said, 'In the name of the Father'; on the second finger, saying, 'and of the Son'; on the third finger, saying, 'and of the Holy Ghost'; then finally on the fourth finger of her left hand, where it would remain, saying, 'Amen'. The fourth finger of the left hand had become the finger on which the wedding ring was worn because it was believed that a certain vein ran from that finger to the heart. The wedding ring itself could be made of gold or silver, but silver was regarded as the true ring by which inward affection was signified.

There then followed the prayers and psalms of the mass. Offerings were made; King Henry honoured the couple with his presence and made an offering of 6s 8d,[6] after which Mary and William received the blessing and left the church as man and wife in the sight of God.

CHAPTER 4

Golden Days, 1520–1522

Resound my voice, ye woods, that hear me plain;

Both hills and vales causing reflexion

William Carey remained in the King's service after his marriage and he played an active part in the revels that made the court of England such an exciting and merry place to be. One such occasion was a reception held in honour of a visit by Charles V.

In fact, the visit was in danger of being cancelled because Charles had been delayed by bad weather and Henry was required to be in France for a meeting with François. In the event, Charles managed to leave port and was met offshore by Wolsey, who escorted him to Dover Castle, where he spent the night. Henry hastened down to meet him. The following day, they rode on to Canterbury together, where Charles met his aunt, Queen Katherine, for the first time in his life. Charles remained at the English court for three days, the leisure hours being passed in the time-honoured fashion of revelry, dancing, banqueting and, of course, jousting.

Three months later, in June 1520, Henry and François met at a summit known as the Field of Cloth of Gold.

Naturally, William Carey was there, accompanied by Mary, who is found in the listings as 'Mastres Carie'. It was all very exciting, but for Mary there was also a touch of apprehension as she went back in her mind to the last time she had crossed to France. She had been young then, little more than a girl, full of idealism as she followed her mistress, Mary Tudor, the French Queen. Then the French Queen had become the White Queen when her husband, the prematurely aged and infirm Louis XII, died after only a few weeks of marriage.

Mary also remembered François, the new King. He was young, exciting, romantic and charming. He and Mary had quickly become lovers and, for Mary, the fairytale had continued, at least until François passed her on to his favourites. Would François remember her? How would he remember her? She need not have worried. King François was a perfect gentleman, in certain situations at least.

The object of the meeting at the Field of Cloth of Gold was to ratify the Treaty of London, which had been brokered by Cardinal Wolsey in October 1518. One of the witnesses of the treaty, which is usually better known as the Treaty of Universal Peace, was Mary's father, Sir Thomas Boleyn. It was, in fact, a non-aggression pact, signed by the major powers of Europe, including England, France and the Habsburg Empire, but smaller states had also signed, such as Denmark, Portugal, Switzerland, and even the Dukes of Gelders and Urbino.

The terms of the treaty were simple: should any of the signatories be threatened or attacked, the victim could appeal to the others who would combine forces to demand the aggressor to withdraw; should they refuse, they would face invasion and war within two months.

It was a good treaty in theory, but, only a year after it had been signed, the Treaty of Universal Peace was in danger of failing. Wolsey worked continuously to rescue it, with meetings being organised between Henry and Charles, and between Henry and François. The first had recently been held; the latter was about to take place at the Field of Cloth of Gold.

Wolsey's endeavour, noble though it was and a masterpiece of diplomacy, was overshadowed by the magnificence of the display that was laid on for the occasion. This had been organised by Mary's father. Sir Thomas understood both Kings well, and he knew that they were rivals in every way beneath the thin veneer of royal brotherhood. The festivities were due to take place in and around Ardres, a small town just beyond the Calais marches on the French side. The town had long fallen into ruin, but it was hastily repaired for the event, its fosses and castle having been rebuilt.

Of course, such a small town could not hold the hundreds of people who made up the entourages of each King, so François's practical solution had been to house everyone in tents in the fields of the Val d'Or, the Golden Vale. Hundreds of colourful tents were erected, each bearing the arms of its occupier. Luxurious pavilions decorated with gold and silver tissue had been prepared, complete with chambers, halls and galleries. A large gilt figure of the Archangel Michael watched over the royal pavilion, the ceiling of which was a skyscape in miniature, complete with stars and the signs of the zodiac.

Since the treaty that each King was to sign had been the result of the hard work of Cardinal Wolsey it was only right that he should open the festivities. It was an occasion fit for a man whose vanity and magnificence were almost legendary. Therefore, on 4 June, escorted by an entourage lead by a hundred archers and fifty gentlemen of his household, the good cardinal made his way towards Ardres, where he was joined by King François. His visit was returned the next day in a series of ceremonies leading up to the meeting of the two Kings on 7 June.

There then followed almost three weeks of festivities. There was dancing, feasting, free-flowing wine from specially plumbed fountains and jousting. The two Kings entertained their courtiers in a wrestling match which, to Henry's chagrin, François won all too easily.

Amid all this merriment Mary was in her element. The colour, the pageantry, the music and excitement enhanced the happiness of a young woman who was in love with life and the fairytale world of the court. Surely the happiest and proudest moment of the entire spectacle must have been when William Carey entered the lists wearing Mary's favours during the seemingly endless series of jousts. William's name is listed among the comers, challengers to those who ran the sets for each joust which, naturally, included the two Kings themselves. Carey was included in the Earl of Devon's band, where his name is given as Sir William Carey. Since he had not actually been knighted, the title had probably been bestowed as a politeness or perhaps even an oversight.

Another cause for excitement was the reunion of the two Boleyn sisters. For it is almost certain that Anne accompanied her mistress, Queen Claude, to the Field of Cloth of Gold. Mary had not seen Anne for almost five years, when the two young women had gone their separate ways. There was much to talk about, not least Mary's delightful new husband. Unfortunately, the reunion was to be very short, but it would be only about eighteen months or so before the Boleyn sisters would be back together again. For as the year 1521 drew to a close, so did Anne Boleyn's time in France. The developing political climate had made it necessary for Sir Thomas to recall his youngest daughter to England.[1]

The timing of Anne's recall coincided with the building and fitting out of ships, the transport of ammunition to Antwerp and the withdrawal of English scholars from the Sorbonne. King François took this to be a sign of an imminent attack on France on the part of the English King.[2] In this he was quite correct, although war was not to break out until the following May. There was, however, another reason behind Anne's departure from France. Negotiations for her proposed marriage to James Butler were beginning to look as though they might bear fruit.

For many years an inheritance dispute had rumbled on between the Boleyns and their Irish cousin, Piers Butler. Mary's uncle, Thomas Howard, the future Duke of Norfolk, suggested an alliance between Piers's heir, James, and Anne as a means to settle matters. As the negotiations continued, Mary and Anne enjoyed another happy reunion. While Mary was kept busy in her post in attendance on Queen Katherine, Anne joined her sister at court; by March 1522 she was officially attached to the royal wardrobe. One of her tasks was to take charge of certain garments and dresses to be used in the Shrovetide festivities of that year.[3]

The Boleyns continued to carve out successful careers at court. Mary was now married to one of Henry's favourites and had become established as a maid of honour to the Queen, while Anne had joined her at court, holding a post in the royal wardrobe. Their mother, Elizabeth, was to be seen from time to time in the service of Queen Katherine. Mary's brother, George, had made his court debut at a mummery during the Christmas revels of 1514–1515. He officially joined Henry's household in 1516 as a page. The Boleyn children were a credit to their father, Sir Thomas, who had proved his worth time and again as a courtier and diplomat, but had also endeared himself to the King through his sporting prowess. The Boleyn star was rising in a way none could have predicted, but it was not to end there. The naughty little cherub, Cupid, had release an arrow whose target could never have been guessed by anyone.

CHAPTER 5

Kindness to a King, Mary & Henry VIII, 1522–1524

A face that should content me wonderous well,

Should not be faire, but lovely to behold:

Of lively look, all grief for to repel;

With right good grace, so would I that it should

Speak, without words, such words as none can tell:

Her tress also should be of crisped gold.

With wit and these perchance I might be tried

And knit again the knot that should not slide

Despite the good intentions expressed in the Treaty of Universal Peace, the cracks had very soon begun to show in the relationship between King Henry of England and King François of France. The situation was not helped by events that were unfolding in Italy.

The Italian wars were a series of conflicts that had begun in 1494 and which involved most of the city and Papal States as well as the major states of western Europe, including France, Spain, the Holy Roman Empire, England and Scotland and the Ottoman Empire. After a short period of uneasy peace, hostilities had once more broken out, the enmity this time being primarily between Charles V and François I. The cause was Charles's elevation as Holy Roman Emperor, a position François had coveted for himself.

Under the terms of the Treaty of Universal Peace, the signatories should have urged the warring sides to settle their differences by negotiation. England, however, chose to back Charles V against King François. Now, in the spring of 1522, Imperial ambassadors had arrived at Henry's court to finalise plans for a joint attack on France. The new relationship was to be sealed by the betrothal of the Emperor Charles to Henry's six-year-old daughter, Princess Mary. For the ambassadors, their stay in England was not all work; their visit coincided with the spectacular Shrovetide festivities.

Shrovetide marked the last occasion for merriment and feasting before the austerity and fasting of Lent. At the English court the event was marked by great celebrations lasting several days. It is probable that Mary Boleyn was one of those who attended the entertainment on 2 March 1522, which took as its theme the anguish of unrequited love. It is possible also that she was one of the spectators at the joust. The crowd watched with excitement as the King rode out, his horse's silver caparison decorated with a wounded heart and the motto *elle mon coeur a navera* – 'she has wounded my heart'. Mary certainly knew the secret of who had wounded the King's heart.

There is no such uncertainty surrounding Mary's whereabouts two days later on Shrove Tuesday. On this day the King, Cardinal Wolsey and the ambassadors had supper together in the great chamber. Then came the entertainment of the *Château Vert* or Green Castle.[1] The chamber was decorated with a great arras, there was a cloth of estate, while large candelabra, each holding thirty-two torches of wax, flooded the chamber with their glowing iridescence.

At the end of the chamber was a castle of green with three towers. The central tower featured a burning cresset, a hanging brazier, while the smaller towers on either side were warded with battlements. The towers were adorned with banners. The first showed three broken hearts, another showed a lady's hand gripping a man's heart, while the third showed a man's heart being turned upside down by a lady's hand.

Within the castle were held, as prisoners, eight ladies of strange names, each reflecting a desirable virtue. The first was Beauty, played by Mary, Duchess of Suffolk. Next was Honour, played by Gertrude Courtenay, Countess of Devon. Anne Boleyn took the part of Perseverance, while Kindness was played by Mary Boleyn. The fifth lady was Constancy, played by Jane Parker, who would one day marry Mary's brother, George. The sixth lady, Bounty, was played by Mistress Browne. Mistress Dannet played Mercy, while the eighth, Pity, was played by a lady whose name is not given. The eight ladies wore gowns of white satin, and featuring her name or 'reason' embroidered in gold. Their head-dresses were Milan bonnets set off by cauls of gold and jewels.

Beneath the castle were another eight 'ladies', in fact played by boys from the Chapel Royal dressed as 'women of India'. Their names were those of undesirable qualities: Danger, Disdain, Jealousy, Unkindness, Scorn, Malebouche (bad-mouthing) and Strangeness (perhaps aloofness or off-handedness). The name of the eighth is lost. The women of India held the virtues as prisoners. Rescue was at hand, however. Eight lords entered, dressed in cloth of gold with great mantle cloaks of blue satin. Their names were Amorous, Nobleness, Youth, Attendance, Loyalty, Pleasure, Gentleness and Liberty and, included among them, was King Henry. They were led by a gentleman dressed in crimson satin, his costume decorated with flames of gold. His name was Ardent Desire, and was almost certainly played by William Cornish, master of the choristers of the Chapel Royal.

Ardent Desire urged the ladies to come down, but Scorn and Disdain refused to allow them, saying they would hold their place. Ardent Desire then declared that the ladies should be won, at which 'battle' was joined. To the sound of a great roar of gunfire from outside, the lords besieged the castle. They advanced, throwing dates, oranges and other fruits as they did so. Finally the castle was won, although Lady Scorn and her company had valiantly defended it with rose water and comfits, bows and balls. The lords then took the ladies of virtue as prisoners and brought them down. They all danced together to the great delight of the guests. After the dance they all took off their masks and sat down to a great banquet.

The theme for the Shrove Tuesday celebrations of 1522 was, as we have seen, unrequited love. However, this theme concealed a secret, for the King had recently fallen in love and, far from being unrequited, it was returned with enthusiasm. It was at about this time, or perhaps a little before, that Mary had captivated the King and become his mistress. She had been the one to have wounded his heart.

Mary Boleyn was not the first woman to have caught the King's eye, of course. Throughout his marriage, all through Katherine's tragic sequence of pregnancies, Henry had taken solace in the arms of other ladies. Most of these liaisons were little more than the means of fulfilling the physical needs of a vigorous man at a time when his pregnant wife had banned him from her bed. All morality aside, it was not unacceptable behaviour for a man in Henry's position and was probably even to be expected in a King. There was little, if any, emotional engagement with any of these women and they posed no danger to the royal marriage. However, other dalliances were not so innocent or inconsequential. In fact, one such entanglement had caused a scandal in 1510; the lady in question being Anne, Lady Hastings, sister of the Duke of Buckingham.

Henry's affair with Lady Hastings took place when Katherine had taken to her chamber in May 1510. To take a mistress under this or any other circumstance was not a difficult thing to do because the arrangements of the royal apartments seemed almost to have been designed to facilitate unfaithfulness. The Queen had her own suite of rooms including a bedchamber, an audience chamber and a withdrawing room. The King enjoyed similar facilities. When Henry succumbed to the charms of the Lady Anne, he used his usual ruse. This was to engage one of his favourites, the obliging Sir William Compton, to act as his go-between.

Sir William's official position at court was Groom of the Stool, an intimate post since it involved attending the King at the closed stool, but the job entailed much more than this. Compton was one of Henry's closest companions, taking care of his papers, his personal finances and even controlling access to the King. Together they had devised a strategy by which Compton would pretend to be enamoured with a lady, whom he would then escort to the King's chambers or, as occasion dictated, allow his London residence to be used as a trysting place.

Unfortunately, this approach had become well known to the rest of the court, so that, when Henry fell for the engaging Lady Hastings and Compton followed his usual routine, everyone knew what was going on. This included the lady's sister, Elizabeth. So concerned was Elizabeth for her family honour that she informed their brother, the Duke of Buckingham.

Edward Stafford, third Duke of Buckingham was renowned for his high self-esteem and fiery temper. He confronted Compton and a furious quarrel ensued. Henry intervened and, to the duke's vexation, came down on Compton's side.

Anne's husband removed his wife to a place far from the court and beyond Henry's reach. Henry, however, took his revenge on Elizabeth and promptly dismissed her from court. This in turn ignited the anger of the Queen, one of whose favourites Elizabeth had been, leading to the first serious quarrel between Henry and Katherine.

It is possible that Henry had also strayed with Jane, or Jeanne, Popincourt,[2] a Frenchwoman originally employed by Henry VII as a companion for his daughters. She had become one of Princess Mary's maids by 1502 and was earning 200 shillings *per annum* ten years later as a member of Queen Katherine's household. In 1514, when Katherine was again lying-in, Jane kept the King company, a service she provided once more, under the same circumstances, the following year. Jane was already notorious, being the acknowledged mistress of the Duc de Longueville. Indeed, she had been censured for her promiscuous behaviour by Louis XII. When Jane finally left the court in May 1515, Henry gave her the substantial sum of £100, payment for services rendered, perhaps. However, the best known of Henry's mistresses was Elizabeth, or Bessie, Blount.

Elizabeth Blount's fame lies mainly in the fact that she gave Henry his first living son, albeit an illegitimate one. Their liaison appears to have begun during the second half of 1518, while their son, Henry Fitzroy, was conceived in September or October of that year. By all accounts this was a short-lived affair and it had come to an end upon the discovery that Elizabeth was pregnant; her last recorded appearance at court was on 3 October at the celebrations held for the treaty of marriage between Henry's daughter, Princess Mary, and the Dauphin François. Henry Fitzroy was born in June 1519 and was recognised by the King shortly afterwards. Elizabeth was married by the following September, although she maintained good relations with King Henry, giving and receiving New Year's gifts.

It is possible that Henry next had a brief dalliance with Arabella Parker, described as 'the wife of a city merchant'. Evidence for this, however, is almost non-existent and it must remain in the realms of speculation. Another suggestion is that it was Margery Parker and not Arabella who had won, although temporarily, the King's affections.

What is slightly more certain is that Henry had a brief affair with Mistress Amadas, the wife of Robert Amadas, who was master of the royal jewel-house at the time. It has been suggested that Sir William Compton's house in Thames Street had once again been used for their rendezvous.[3] If Mistress Amadas had been Henry's mistress, it was another short-lived affair for, not long afterwards, King Henry was enjoying the charms of Mary Boleyn.

Later portraits of Henry VIII show him to be probably the least desirable of men. Grossly overweight, his face bloated, his eyes squeezed to mean little windows through which only his cruelty and meanness shone clearly. It is all too easy to forget that the youthful Henry was a most attractive man, one whom women would desire even if he weren't the King. The Venetian ambassador, Ludovico Falias, left a remarkable pen portrait of Henry which, although it slightly postdates his relationship with Mary, nevertheless gives us a very good impression of Henry VIII in the prime of his life:

In this eighth Henry, God combined such corporal and mental beauty, as not merely to surprise but to astound all men. Who could fail to be struck with admiration on perceiving the lofty position of so glorious a Prince to be in such accordance with his stature, giving manifest proof of that intrinsic mental superiority which is inherent to him? His face is angelic rather than handsome; his head imperial (Cesarina) and bald, and he wears a beard, contrary to English custom. Who would not be amazed when contemplating such singular corporal beauty, coupled with such bold address, adapting itself with the greatest ease to every manly exercise. He sits his horse well, and manages him yet better; he jousts and wields his spear, throws the quoit, and draws the bow, admirably; plays at tennis most dexterously; and nature having endowed him in youth with such gifts, he was not slow to enhance, preserve, and augment them with all industry and labour. It seeming to him monstrous for a Prince not to cultivate moral and intellectual excellence, so from childhood he applied himself to grammatical studies, and then to philosophy and holy writ, thus obtaining the reputation of a lettered and excellent Prince. Besides the Latin and his native tongue, he learned Spanish, French, and Italian. He is kind and affable, full of graciousness and courtesy, and liberal;

particularly so to men of science (virtuosi) whom he is never weary of obliging.[4]

How, then, did Mary Boleyn fare against this monument to manly virtue and beauty, this intellectual giant? It has been implied that Mary was not very bright, or, at least, not the intellectual equal of her sister. As such Thomas Boleyn 'clearly recognised that she [Anne] had a brighter intellect that her sister Mary'.[5] This may be so, but it is hard to imagine a man of Henry's intellect being attracted to a stupid woman, much less keeping her as his mistress for any length of time.

Tradition has it that Mary was the most beautiful of the Boleyn sisters. Even she, however, did not conform to the Tudor ideal of feminine beauty, which preferred pale skin, blue eyes and blonde hair. One portrait of Mary, although it is of doubtful authenticity, shows her to have a rounder and softer face than that of her sister. Her complexion is creamy, her eyes brown and, although her hair is hidden beneath her gabled hood, its colour is suggested by the shade of her eyebrows, which hint at a rich auburn or a chestnut brown. Her portrait suggests that she was more plump than otherwise, and the way she holds her head, her straight gaze and the hint of a smile evoke a certain air of self-assuredness that perhaps intrigued the King.

Mary's reputation earned in France did not appear to bother Henry unduly, and it might be that he simply wanted to retain her as little more that a sex object in the way he had with other women before her. If so, her reputation worked to her advantage as Sir William Compton once again played his part and approached Mary on the King's behalf. This, however, was not how the affair would work out. In fact, Henry's relationship with Mary Boleyn would turn out to be longer than that of any of his other mistresses; indeed, its duration would exceed that of some of his later marriages.

It is not known exactly when Henry's eye fell upon Mary Boleyn. Naturally, their romance was conducted with the utmost discretion and it remained unacknowledged by Henry at the time. This makes it difficult to pinpoint the timing of the relationship. It is probably safe to guess, however, that it coincided with a series of grants and awards made by Henry to Mary's friends and family. One person who might have benefited from Mary's influence was Thomas Gardiner, who was appointed to Tynemouth Priory.[6] Gardiner was the son of William Gardiner, who had married the illegitimate daughter of Jasper Tudor, Henry's great uncle.

More significant are the awards made to Mary's husband, William Carey, between the years 1522 and 1525. If these are anything to go by, the affair had probably begun by February 1522, for on the fifth of that month Carey was appointed keeper of the manor and estate of New Hall in Essex and of the King's wardrobe there. He was made bailiff of the manors of New Hall, Boreham, Walkeforde Hall and Powers, also in Essex, with sixty cartloads of firewood annually for the wardrobe and powers to let the premises to farm and to engage labourers to work in the King's garden and orchard.[7]

It is interesting to see New Hall listed among these grants. It had previously belonged to Sir Thomas Boleyn as part of his legacy from the Ormond estates. Boleyn had sold it to King Henry in 1517 and the King changed its name to Beaulieu, although the name was not to last very long. Now it was to be administered by his son-in-law. Under normal circumstances the keeper would be allocated specific chambers in which he and his family would live. With New Hall it was a different matter; William and Mary Carey would be allowed to live there as though they owned it.[8]

In July 1522 William Carey and one of the King's pages, William West, was granted the wardship of Thomas Sharpe of Canterbury, described as an 'idiot', and custody of his lands.[9] The administration of these lands led to a substantial income and opened the way for Carey to become a very rich man. The following year Carey received an annuity of fifty marks[10] and was made chief steward, receiver and bailiff of the manor of Writtell and keeper of Writtell Park in Essex, with various fees and herbage and pannage.

While William Carey was well rewarded for his acquiescence in the matter of his wife's relationship with the King, his father-in-law was even more so. Sir Thomas Boleyn was made treasurer of the household on 24 April 1522. Five days later he and Mary's brother, George, were jointly awarded various offices at Tunbridge, and well as the receivership of Bransted and the keepership of Penshurst.

Tunbridge and Penshurst had been among the properties of Edward Stafford, third Duke of Buckingham, the brother of Henry's former mistress, Lady Hastings. Buckingham had been executed by Henry on 17 May 1521 on charges of treason. However, it is probable that his Plantagenet blood and his claim to the throne, which was better than Henry's, were also contributing factors. Nevertheless, Buckingham's estates were forfeited to the crown; Henry was free to keep them for himself or to grant them to favourite courtiers, as in this case. It is possible that Henry used Penshurst, which is very close to Hever, as a place of assignation during his affair with Mary.

In 1523 Henry acquired a ship called the *Mary Boleyn*. She had a displacement of 100 tons, was captained by William Symonds and had a crew of seventy-nine men. However, Henry did not name the ship after his mistress as has sometimes been thought. Instead, he bought her from Sir Thomas Boleyn at the cost of £521 8s 6½d.[11] He would also acquire her sister ship, the *Anne Boleyn*. The Boleyn honours did not end there. In April 1523 Sir Thomas became a Knight of the Garter.

CHAPTER 6

A Turning Point, 1524

Once, as methought, fortune me kiss'd,

And bade me ask what I thought best,

And I should have it as me list,

Therewith to set my heart at rest.

Mary was presumably present at the joust held in the spring of 1524, when Henry wore a new suit of armour, which he had designed himself. Eager to show it off to his courtiers, he caused quite a stir as he entered the lists against the Duke of Suffolk, but as the jousting got underway the King forgot to lower his visor. Suffolk, encased in his own helm, was unable to see the crowd waving frantically for him to stop, and he was deaf to the cries of 'Hold, hold!' As they thundered towards each other the duke's lance struck the King's helm and shattered. Splinters flew in all directions and some went into Henry's headpiece. The King, bruised, blood pouring down his face, picked himself up and laughed off the incident. He had survived what could have been a terrible accident. However, the incident made him think. What would have happened if Suffolk's lance had struck him in the face? Without a doubt it would have meant certain death, but what would have happened to the kingdom? Was the Tudor dynasty to die with Henry VIII? These unpleasant questions brought home to Henry just how vulnerable his position was in the absence of an heir.

King Henry's relationship with Mary, therefore, came at an important juncture in his life. The King was undergoing a transformation. He now began to look at his life differently and his focus settled upon his marriage to Katherine of Aragon.

In the early years of their marriage Henry had been passionately in love with his Queen. It is easy to see why. Katherine was intelligent. Her education, adhering strictly to a Catholic Christian perspective, was based on the Bible certainly, but she also studied classic texts in both Latin and the vernacular. The humanist approach came from the tuition of Alessandro and Antonio Geraldini. Katherine was taught modern languages, although she seems not to have mastered English terribly well at first. As such, she was more than a match for Henry intellectually and fully able to hold her own in conversation with him.

Moreover, as a young woman, Katherine had been very attractive. Small and delicate, she was renowned for her translucent, English rose complexion and very long auburn hair. In contrast to the sallow creaminess of her Spanish ladies, Katherine's looks betrayed her English descent – her grandmother, after whom she was named, was Catalina, or Katherine, of Lancaster, daughter of John of Gaunt and his second wife, Constanza. Catalina had married Enrique III of Castile. As such, Katherine was the perfect bride and Queen for Henry VIII, even being descended from the English royal family. However, Katherine was unable to fulfil her duty as Queen in one vital respect: she could not give Henry his much needed son.

Henry VIII was acutely aware that the Tudor dynasty had been built upon foundations of sand. His father had not acquired the throne by right of inheritance, but only by right of conquest. It was vital that each Tudor King should produce sons in order to secure the throne and prevent a resurgence of the dynastic wars that had torn the English aristocracy apart. The wars between the Houses of York and Lancaster were not distant memories; there was every chance that they would reignite. Henry VIII, like his father before him, knew that some of their most powerful subjects had a greater claim to wear the crown than they did. The affair of the Duke of Buckingham had been a stark reminder to Henry of this very fact.

Buckingham was a direct descendant of Edward III through his son, Thomas of Woodstock and was of the legitimate line, rather than the illegitimate one from which the Tudors descended. At his trial it was stated that he had listened rather too eagerly to Nicholas Hopkins, a Carthusian monk, who had been making political prophecies since 1512. One of his prophecies stated that Buckingham would one day be King. Buckingham believed that the Tudor dynasty had been cursed by God as a result of the judicial murder of the Earl of Warwick in 1499, notwithstanding his own participation in the earl's trial, and that Henry's lack of male issue had been proof of this.

In such a superstitious age, anyone seeking support for such a prophecy had only to look at Katherine's gynaecological record. It was a catalogue of miscarriages, stillbirths and babies who were born only to die within a few hours or days. One son, named Henry after his father, was born on New Year's Day 1511 but he had died shortly afterwards. A daughter, Princess Mary, was born on 18 February 1516. Then, in November 1518, Katherine's final pregnancy resulted in a stillborn daughter.

Throughout this time, Henry had clung to the hope that Katherine would give him a living son. As the years went by even he was forced to admit that his greatest wish would probably not be granted. At times he sank into the depths of despair.

The respective ages of the King and Queen, of little consequence in the early days of their marriage, now took on a new significance. Katherine was six years older than Henry. While he was still in the first flush of youth, or believed himself to be, Katherine was advancing steadily towards middle age. Moreover, her many pregnancies had taken their toll on her looks. She had become overweight, King François described her as 'deformed', by which he meant fat, and she was no longer the attractive woman she had been. Had she given Henry a son, this would have been of no consequence. However, for all her pregnancies, Queen Katherine had managed to present Henry with only one child that lived: Mary. Now her childbearing days had come to an end. Now it looked as though the throne would pass to Princess Mary and not to the son the King had so desperately longed for.

Henry, anxious that this should not happen, seems to have considered legitimising his son, Henry Fitzroy, and placing him above any child he might have except for a legitimate son. With this in view, Henry created the boy Duke of Richmond and Somerset, but it was not long before his thoughts took another, more dangerous, turn. He decided he would repudiate Katherine and take another wife, someone who would give him sons.

Vague rumours had already circulated that Henry would seek to annul his marriage, replacing Katherine with another. As early as 1514, during the negotiations for the marriage of Henry's sister to King Louis XII of France, the Venetian ambassador had noted that 'the King of England meant to repudiate his present wife, the daughter of the King of Spain and his brother's widow, because he is unable to have children by her'. He added that Henry had intended to marry 'the daughter of the French Duke of Bourbon' instead. The matter arose again in 1522 or 1523.[1] Clearly these rumours had been false.

While it is not possible to pinpoint the exact date, Henry would not actively seek to replace Katherine until after June

1525, which was when he elevated Henry Fitzroy to the peerage. Moreover, when Henry did initiate proceedings to dissolve his marriage, it was not in order to replace Katherine with a daughter of the Duke of Bourbon. Still, such rumours do show that Henry's situation was of interest to those beyond the court and had become the subject of speculation.

Perhaps Henry confided his worries to Mary. Perhaps he wished with all his heart that he could make her his wife. Alas, that was not to be. Although it was possible for spouses to obtain separations, they could not remarry. This had happened to the poet Thomas Wyatt, whose unhappy marriage to Elizabeth Brooke was not helped by the fact that she was an adulteress. After his separation, Wyatt was free to take a mistress, with whom he had an illegitimate son, although the couple were forbidden ever to marry.

Had Henry wished to take Mary as his wife he would have been forced to dissolve his marriage to Katherine of Aragon and also Mary's to William Carey. As it happened, he would find a way to annul his marriage to Katherine, but when he did so, it was not in order to marry Mary but her sister, Anne.

Just when Mary's relationship with the King reached its conclusion is, like its naissance, shrouded in mystery. All that can be said is that William Carey received his last royal grant in 1526. This, as will by shown, coincides with the birth of Mary's son, Henry Carey, a child whose paternity is open to debate. It is probably safe to speculate, however, that the end of Mary's time as Henry's mistress corresponded with, or was even precipitated by, the rise of Anne Boleyn.

Yet, to make matters even more uncertain, it cannot be said when King Henry first became interested in Anne Boleyn. Since her return from France at the end of 1521 Anne had established a presence at court as one of Queen Katherine's maids of honour. She had taken part, alongside her sister and other beauties of the court, at the *Château Vert* pageant held at Shrovetide 1522. Nevertheless, negotiations for Anne's marriage to James Butler were ongoing, although they eventually came to nothing.

Anne then captured the attention of Henry Percy, future sixth Earl of Northumberland. This would have been a perfectly suitable match for Anne, who would eventually have become Countess of Northumberland. According to George Cavendish, gentleman usher to Cardinal Wolsey and, later, his biographer, Henry had ordered the cardinal to intervene and put an end to the courtship because of his own interest in Anne.[2] However, this could not be the case because the timing is incorrect. It is more probable that Henry wanted to ensure that existing plans for the match between James Butler and Anne, as well as that between Lord Percy and his betrothed, Mary Talbot, should not be jeopardised.

Henry Percy was betrothed to Mary Talbot in January or February 1524. Shortly before this date, Sir Thomas Boleyn had returned home from a diplomatic mission abroad. He took Anne away from court, probably to Hever. It had been conjectured[3] that Sir Thomas was punishing his daughter, and that he was effectively banishing her from court, or else he was protecting her from the attentions of a lecherous King; anxious, perhaps to save her from Mary's fate.

Whatever the case, Anne returned to court in 1525. She was now in her early twenties and, although not considered beautiful, she had wit, charm, a certain elegance that had been cultivated at the French court, and she was smoulderingly sexy. It was at some point during this year that Henry 'noticed' Anne.

The creation of her father as Viscount Rochford on 18 June possibly marks the point at which Mary's reign as mistress entered its final phase. It was also at about this time that Mary, who had now acquired the title of Lady Rochford, became pregnant. It could be speculated that, as the pregnancy progressed, Mary became 'difficult' and was reluctant to allow the King near her, inadvertently forcing him to look elsewhere for solace. Thus began the ascent of Anne Boleyn.

The conclusion of Mary's relationship with Henry was marked in a most public way at the Shrove Tuesday joust held at Greenwich in 1526. For those who had eyes to see the signs were there that the King's affections had transferred to a new lady, even if her identity had not yet been guessed. The joust was led by Henry on the one side and his old friend, Henry Courtenay, now the Marquis of Exeter, on the other. The King was magnificent in cloth of gold and silver, richly embroidered with a man's heart enclosed within in a press and encircled by a flame. The motto was *Declare ie nose* – 'declare I dare not'.[4] Henry was taking the part of a tortured lover in what could well have been his first public declaration of love for Anne Boleyn.

According to Sander,[5] the Elizabethan recusant living in exile, Mary Boleyn now understood that Henry preferred Anne to her. In her pique she went to Queen Katherine and urged her to remain cheerful. For, while the King was in love with her sister, he would never marry her because his relationship with the family made such a match impossible under ecclesiastical law. 'The king himself will not deny it, and I will assert it publicly while I live; now, as he may not marry my sister, so neither will he put your majesty away.' The Queen then thanked Mary and replied that whatever she might do or say would be at the direction of her lawyers.

Here, Sander is describing a scene that, in all probability, never took place. Moreover, he is anticipating actions on Henry's part that even the King was not yet contemplating. Rather than looking upon Anne as a future wife, Henry simply regarded her as a prospective mistress, a pleasing diversion. Still, the words attributed to Mary by Sander are prophetic. When the time came for Henry to reconsider the nature of his relationship with Anne, his prior relationship with Mary would prove to be a serious impediment, one that would require a papal dispensation to give it an air of legality. Then, on a more sinister note, when Henry decided to rid himself of Anne, his relationship with Mary would be used as a valuable weapon in his armoury.

The end of Mary's relationship with Henry is marked, like its beginning, with grants to her husband. On 12 May 1526 Carey is made keeper of the manor, garden and tower of Pleasance in Greenwich and of East Greenwich Park, with fees out of the issues of Kent.[6]

It has been suggested that Greenwich was one of the places Henry and Mary would come together. The clergyman and historian L'Estrange notes that Henry had repaired or rebuilt the 'castle' on the hill at Greenwich, which he would sometimes use for the storage of wine 'and sometimes for the keeping of other delicacies'. Was one such 'delicacy' Mary Boleyn? He continues:

> The king ... having Flamock with him in his barge, going from Westminster to Greenwich to visit a fair lady whom the king loved, who was lodged in the tower of the park, the king coming within sight of the tower, and being disposed to be merry, said, 'Flamock, let us run...'[7]

Also on 12 May 1526, William Carey was granted the keepership of the manor and park of Ditton in Buckinghamshire, with all the foreign woods belonging to the same, with 3d a day.[8] It is very possible that we see in these grants a token of gratitude, a fitting reward to a man who had worn his cuckold's horns so gracefully.

As Mary's star was eclipsed by the increasing brilliance of Anne's, it is interesting to contrast how each Boleyn sister responded to Henry's advances. Mary had thrown herself into the affair with a passion. As Starkey puts it, 'Mary... had been in love with Henry, and, being in love, had done what came naturally.'[9]

Anne's response was somewhat different. She rejected out of hand the idea of being Henry's mistress. Henry's response, and the course of his thinking, can be traced in the seventeen love letters he wrote to Anne. These are undated, but internal and circumstantial evidence suggests that his courtship began in earnest at Shrovetide 1526.

When Anne rejected the King's proposal to become his mistress she left court and returned to Hever. Henry then offered her a post similar to that of the *maîtresse en titre* so familiar to the Kings of France. Anne rejected this also. Henry pressed on, managing to offend her as he did so; Anne told him that she had given her maidenhead into her husband's hands. This simple but earnest statement had a remarkable effect on Henry. Suddenly he knew that he could not live without her. At the same time he realised that his need to remarry in order to have sons could be satisfied just as well by marrying Anne as it could by marrying some foreign princess. When Henry at last offered Anne the chance to be his wife and his Queen, he got the response he had been looking for.

CHAPTER 7

King Henry VIII's Children?
1524–1526

Alas! poor man, what hap have I,

That must forbear that I love best!

Mary Boleyn was King Henry's mistress for a period of more than three years. Dating from at least Shrovetide 1522 to the autumn of 1525, it lasted even longer than Henry's later marriages; the exception being his marriage to Katherine Parr, which lasted four years and ended with the death of the King. Its duration makes it highly unusual in the history of Henry VIII's extra martial affairs. Yet there is one aspect to the relationship that makes it unique: the fact that Henry did not abandon Mary when she became pregnant.

Mary, in fact, was pregnant twice during the time that she was Henry's mistress. The eldest child, Katherine, was born in 1524. The year of her birth is easy to establish from a portrait of her which was painted in 1562. This notes that the sitter was thirty-eight years of age at the time, giving her a birth date of 1524.

Mary's second child, a son whom she named Henry, was born on 4 March 1526. As has been established, King Henry had, by this time, transferred his interest from Mary to her sister, Anne. However, a child born in March would have been conceived in June of the previous year when Henry had not yet discarded Mary. The question must be asked, then: was Henry VIII the father of Mary's two children?

Perhaps the first thing to note in answer to this is that Henry did not acknowledge Katherine and Henry Carey as he had done with Henry Fitzroy, the son he had by Elizabeth Blount. The fact that Elizabeth's boy was given the name of Fitzroy, literally the 'son of the King' is testament to Henry's acceptance of him as his son. Rather, Mary's son and daughter were given her husband's name, Carey. It would appear, then, that they were not the King's children, but that their father was, in fact, William Carey.

Perhaps the most compelling argument against Mary's children having been fathered by Henry VIII is the apparent low fertility of the King. Of the eight women with whom he had sexual relations, or was presumed to have had, only four managed to conceive and to carry their baby successfully to term. Katherine of Aragon had six pregnancies during the first ten years of her marriage to Henry VIII; most had resulted in miscarriages and stillbirths so that, by 1524, when Henry stopped sleeping with her, Katherine had produced only one surviving child: Princess Mary.

With Anne Boleyn it was to be a similar story. While there are no records of stillbirths, she did miscarry at least twice and her marriage with Henry also produced only one child: Princess Elizabeth.

After Anne, Henry married Jane Seymour. Once again, the marriage produced only one child, the future Edward VI. However, because Jane died shortly after giving birth to her son, no real judgement can be made regarding the fruitfulness of this marriage; Jane might have gone on to have more children had she lived.

Henry's next wife, Anne of Cleves, gave him no children. His fifth wife, Katherine Howard, also gave him no children, although the French ambassador, Marillac, reported rumours that she had conceived early in her relationship with the King.[1] Henry's sixth and last wife, Katherine Parr, certainly had no children by him.

This is a not a good record, especially given the success of some of the families these women came from. Perhaps there was a physical reason for Henry's poor performance. It has often been said, and was once accepted as fact, that Henry had contracted some form of venereal disease which had affected his potency. If so, one possible source for this might have been Mary Boleyn. She had been mistress to François I of France, though for only a short time. François was known to have been heavily infected with syphilis and, in turn, could have infected Mary. If so, she could have carried the disease to Henry.

One argument put forward in support of Henry having been infected with syphilis centred upon the ulcer on his leg. This had caused him trouble since 1528 or so and has been seen as a symptom of syphilis in times past. However, it is now known that Henry had never been treated for the disease. In addition, the leg ulcer has been identified as a symptom of osteomyelitis, which probably resulted from a fall from his horse. There is nothing to support the hypothesis that either Mary or Henry VIII had syphilis or any other form of venereal disease.

There is every chance, however, that Henry's fertility problems arose from psychological causes. Henry, so anxious to have a son, was prevented by that very anxiety from doing that which was necessary in order to father one. The one exception to this, although it does not defeat the argument, is the case of Anne of Cleves. Henry claimed that he could not make love to her because he found her so unattractive. He also suspected that she was not a virgin when she came to him; perhaps he worried that she might have compared him unfavourably with other men.

During his short marriage to Anne of Cleves, Henry was eager to point out that he was perfectly capable of making love to any other woman, just not with her. However, was this really the case? Anne Boleyn is said to have told her sister-in-law, the Viscountess Rochford, that the King was incapable of satisfying a woman, having neither the skill nor the potency. The matter was raised later at the trial of Anne's brother, George, Viscount Rochford. He was handed a piece of paper upon which the question of Henry's sexual ability was written. Although he was told not to read it out aloud to the court, he did so, and this was said to have sealed his fate.

Anne Boleyn's comment is telling. It suggests that Henry's problem was impotence, or erectile dysfunction. One of the causes of impotence is anxiety or stress. Henry was anxious to have sons, as we know. His failure to father one was a cause of some stress and this only worsened as time went on. However, when Henry was with his mistresses, it was a different matter. With no pressure to produce an heir by them, he could relax in their company. In so doing, he was able to function normally with the result that they conceived. Henry might have had other children with Elizabeth Blount, for instance, had he not discarded her at the first signs of her pregnancy. As it was, Elizabeth gave the King his first son whom he named Henry Fitzroy in acknowledgement of his paternity.

A conversation that took place between Henry and the Imperial ambassador, Eustache Chapuys, in April 1533 is very revealing of Henry's attitude at the time.[2] This occurred at the height of Henry's attempt to dissolve his marriage to Katherine of Aragon. Chapuys had pointed out to Henry that most people abroad were on Katherine's side, adding that there were those within his own kingdom who also supported Katherine, unless they had been won over. At this point Henry, anxious to divert the conversation, told Chapuys that he wished to have a successor to his kingdom. Chapuys reminded Henry that he already had a successor, a daughter who was more than capable and who, he added, was of childbearing age. He reminded the King that he had received the principal title to his realm through the female line and that nature seemed to oblige him to restore it to Princess Mary. This was certainly true. Henry's father had married Elizabeth of York, the daughter of Edward IV, to lend legitimacy to the new Tudor regime. Henry dismissed this, saying that he knew better than his daughter and asserted that he wanted to have children. At this point Chapuys, who certainly sailed close to the wind at times, remarked that Henry was not sure of having them. Furious, Henry rounded on the ambassador, 'Am I not a man like other men?' he yelled, adding that Chapuys was not privy to all his secrets. Chapuys took this to mean that Henry's wife, Anne Boleyn, was pregnant.

This exchange tells us two things about Henry. Firstly, Henry was extremely sensitive about his inability to father a son and here we find out what was at the root of it: he did not believe that a woman could wear the crown after him. Secondly, no matter how many children he had, they did not count unless they were boys. Naturally, he hoped that the baby Anne was carrying was a boy. As it turned out, the baby was a girl, Elizabeth.

Yet, for all his difficulty in fathering a legitimate heir, Henry did manage to produce at least one illegitimate son. This was, of course, Henry Fitzroy. Since Henry acknowledged him, there is no need to try to establish his paternity. However, Fitzroy might not have been Henry's only illegitimate child.

Ethelreda or Audrey Harington is understood to have been Henry's child, passed off as the daughter of his tailor, John Malte. Certainly there is mention of 'John Malte, tailor, and Awdrye his base daughter' among the purchasers of crown lands in January 1547.³ Ethelreda went on to marry John Harington, a courtier and writer who studied under the famous Thomas Tallis. As a result of his marriage, Harington received dissolved monastic lands in Berkshire and Somerset.

Harington belonged to the staunchly Yorkist family who prospered under Edward IV and were vigorously supported by Richard III who, while still Duke of Gloucester, helped them resist attempts by the Stanley family to take their castle of Hornsby. Following Richard's defeat at Bosworth, much of the Haringtons' property was forfeited to the crown.⁴ Yet, despite his family's loyalty to the House of York, John Harington was favoured by Henry VIII. This might have been due to his wife's relationship to the King. As such, there is a hint of support for the theory that Ethelreda was Henry's illegitimate daughter. Ethelreda and John attended Princess Elizabeth when she was imprisoned in the Tower and the couple flourished following Elizabeth's accession. John Harington continued as a royal favourite following the death of his wife prior to 1559.

Next is Thomas Stucley who was born about 1520 to Jane, the wife of Sir Hugh Stucley of Affeton Castle in Devon. Contemporary rumours held that he was an illegitimate son of Henry VIII, but there appears to be little evidence to support this.

Another alleged natural son is John Perrot, born about 1528, Perrot's candidature is largely due to the work of Robert Naunton, who was writing in 1630.[5] Naunton wrote that Perrot's father, Thomas, was a gentleman of the privy chamber who married a lady of great honour. This he found to be presumptuous. Going further, he added that Perrot's pictures, qualities, gesture and voice all reminded people of the late King, who continued to live in the memory of a great many people. This suggested to Naunton that Perrot was Henry's illegitimate child.

That Henry was the true father of Stukley and Perrot has, however, been discredited. Still, Naunton's conjecture does serve to show how readily people believed in Henry's sexual prowess and their eager acceptance of any theory regarding his illegitimate issue.

Another possibility is the poet and playwright Richard Edwardes, who went on to become a gentleman of the Chapel Royal. Edwardes is generally thought to have been born in 1523; that is, during Henry's relationship with Mary. According to his biographer,[6] given his family's circumstances, the fact that Richard went to Oxford and his subsequent career could only be accounted for by his being Henry's son. This is a very speculative viewpoint which excludes the possibility that the boy might have had patrons other than his supposed father.

Of all the people mentioned so far, only Ethelreda Harington finds some support for her claim to be an illegitimate child of Henry VIII. Of course, because Henry chose to acknowledge only one of his natural children, any attempt to prove that he was the father of any given child must rest upon speculation or, at best, circumstantial evidence.

This applies equally to the children of Mary Boleyn. Because Henry did not acknowledge Katherine and Henry Carey, there is no tangible proof to say that he was their father. However, when circumstantial evidence is taken into account, the chances that Mary's children were fathered by Henry rather than William Carey greatly increase.

In the case of Katherine Carey, it has been established that she was born in 1524. Katherine was appointed maid of honour to Henry's fourth Queen, Anne of Cleves, in November 1539 at the age of fifteen, the appropriate age for such a post.[7]

Katherine married Francis Knollys on 26 April 1540, and their first child, Henry, was born on 12 April the following year.[8] While, in the case of child marriages, the couple did not live together until they were deemed of age, Katherine clearly entered into full marital relations with her husband as soon as they married, strongly suggesting that she was considered mature enough.

Katherine went into the service of Queen Elizabeth. Like Ethelreda Harington she was always one of the Queen's favourites and theirs was a friendship that had probably begun in childhood.[9] When, in 1556, Katherine and Sir Francis left England as part of the exodus of the Marian exiles, her departure greatly distressed Elizabeth, who wrote an emotional farewell letter to her signed *cor rotto* ('broken heart'). The duration of their exile is not known, but Katherine was appointed as a waged lady of the bedchamber by Elizabeth, who was by that time Queen, in January 1559. When Katherine became ill, Elizabeth visited her often and was heartbroken when she died. Queen Elizabeth gave Katherine a funeral of such magnificence that it can only be described as 'royal', with a cost of £640 2s 11d.[10] It was said that the funeral furniture was so valuable that it caused a dispute between the abbey and the college of heralds.[11] Such closeness between the Queen and Katherine could be explained by the fact that they were cousins. A better explanation, especially considering the sum Elizabeth spent on Katherine's funeral, would be that they were, in fact, half-sisters.

Circumstantial evidence can also be offered in the case of Mary's son, Henry Carey. For example, a report written in November 1531 by the Venetian ambassador, Ludovico Falias, mentions that Henry had a 'natural son born to him of the widow of one of his Peers; a youth of great promise, so much does he resemble his father'. This might refer to Henry Carey, since Mary was a widow at the time this report was written. It is equally possible that the son referred to is

Henry Fitzroy, whose mother, Elizabeth Blount, had been widowed the previous year. Since Fitzroy was known to be the King's son, no real revelation is being made here.

Henry Carey's contemporaries, such as Ludovico Falias, thought that he resembled the King, but this is hardly conclusive. Another piece of evidence at least mentions the boy by name. In April 1535, John Hale, vicar of Isleworth, suggested that Henry Carey was the King's son: 'Moreover, Mr. Skydmore did show to me young Master Care, saying that he was our sovereign Lord the King's son by our sovereign Lady the Queen's sister, whom the Queen's grace might not suffer to be in the Court.'[12]

Hale's account is typical of contemporary gossip spread primarily by supporters of Katherine of Aragon, and who asserted that Henry Carey was the King's bastard son. Such gossip might have had some foundation in fact. Hale was certainly right in one respect: at this point Anne and Mary had become estranged and Mary was forbidden the court. John Hale was executed shortly afterwards for denying the King's supremacy.[13]

One of the main arguments against Henry's paternity of Henry Carey is that the child was born after the King's relationship with Mary had ended. On the other hand, as has been shown, the boy was born in March 1526. This means that he was probably conceived during the June of the previous year at which time the relationship was still ongoing. Clearly this in itself does little to substantiate the argument in favour of Henry Carey having been fathered by the King, but when this and other circumstantial evidence is added to documentary evidence, the case is somewhat strengthened.

It is significant that most of the royal grants awarded to William Carey are concentrated on the dates that coincide with the birth of Mary's children. Therefore, on 15 June 1524 William Carey, described as squire of the body, is made keeper of the manor of Wansted in Essex, with 2d a day out of the issues of the manor. This grant was held jointly with John Parker, a page of the privy chamber.[14] Three days later, on 18 June, William and Mary Carey are awarded the grant of manors of Stanford Rivers, Traceys and Suttons, and appurtenances there and in High Ongar in Essex.[15]

As can be seen, the timing of these royal grants corresponds with the approximate date of Katherine Carey's birth. It is difficult to discount the possibility that they were awarded to William Carey as incentives to accept paternity of his wife's daughter.

The same thing occurs in 1526 to coincide with the impending birth of Henry Carey. On 20 February William Carey is granted the manors of Parva Brickhill, Burton and Essington in Buckinghamshire, with licence to hold fairs and markets and sundry other liberties in Parva Brickhill and Buckingham.[16] This grant was made just two weeks before the birth of Henry Carey. It could be argued that, as with the grants awarded at the time of Katherine Carey's birth, this one had to do with appeasing Mary's husband

and persuading him to accept paternity of the child. This is all the more so when it is realised that they are not the simple stewardships or keeperships normally given out to courtiers, but the means of making a substantial living.

Moreover, William Carey was among those retained in the King's service following the enactment of the Eltham Ordinances in January 1526. This, as with the purge a few years previously, had trimmed the number of minions surrounding the King. Although Henry had almost certainly put Mary aside by this time, he would still want to be generous to her if he felt that the child she was carrying was his. To retain her husband in his post was one way of ensuring financial security and stability for the family as well as providing a means of rewarding Carey for his complaisance. For, even though he no longer wanted Mary as his mistress, Henry was to retain a fondness for her.

Another argument often put forward against Henry being the father of Mary Boleyn's two children is that he had a penchant for being the only man in the life of his significant other. This is certainly true when it came to his wives. One case in point is that of Anne of Cleves. One of the reasons Henry cited for his inability to make love to her was his suspicion that she was not a virgin when she came to him. When, on the morning after the wedding, Cromwell asked him if he liked his new wife any better, Henry had replied, 'Nay, my Lord, much worse, for by her breasts and belly she should be no maid.'[17] Ironically, Henry announced that he had 'left her as good a maid as he found her'.[18] Later, when the Cleves marriage was annulled, the ex-Queen was made to write to her brother assuring him that her body 'remaineth in the integrity which I brought into this realm'.[19] Of course, in Anne of Cleves's case there was more to Henry's dislike of her than the suspicion of her not being pure. It was, however, a good excuse to cover his inability to have sex with her as well as to rid himself of an unwanted bride.

Another example is Henry's 'jewel for womanhood', Katherine Howard. Whether she had willingly taken lovers before her marriage is debatable. What is clear is that she was not a virgin when she married Henry, nor did she remain faithful to him after their wedding. When he found out about her adultery, 'the King's heart was pierced with pensiveness, so that it was long before he could utter his sorrow; and finally, with plenty of tears, (which was strange in his courage), opened the same'.[20]

That Henry demanded exclusive access to the women in his life is certainly true when it came to his wives. When it came to his mistresses, however, it was a different matter. Anne, Lady Hastings was certainly married at the time of Henry's dalliance with her, while Jane Popincourt was the celebrated mistress of the Duc de Loungueville. What, then, of Mary? How exclusive was her relationship with the King? As we know, Mary Boleyn was married throughout her lengthy relationship with Henry. It is possible that the Carey marriage was non-sexual; that Mary and William, although cohabiting, did not sleep together as man and wife. Alternatively, Mary might have been clever enough to know how to control her own fertility. Certainly, there were means available to ladies who did not wish to conceive. These were known to Mary's cousin, Katherine Howard, who famously stated that 'a woman might meddle with a man and yet conceive no child unless she would herself'.[21]

Among these methods[22] are breast-feeding after giving birth, coitus interruptus, 'hard pissing', condoms made of skin, animal gut or linen, placing a cockerel's testicles under the bed or using beeswax to seal the neck of the womb. In the event of an unwanted pregnancy, rue, marigold, savin, tansy, mandrake and bark of white poplar were all known to bring on an abortion. Since it was believed that the foetus was soulless until eighty days after conception, or at the 'quickening', early abortions were free of ethical concerns.

If Mary had used such methods, they clearly did not work on every occasion. On the other hand, there is always the possibility that her pregnancies were not accidents, but planned, as far as they could be, to ensure that Henry might at least have children other than Henry Fitzroy to act as spares in the event that he had no legitimate sons. They also served to show, if nothing else, that it was not Henry's fault that the palace corridors did not echo with the patter of tiny feet, which probably gave a much-needed boost to his ego.

If Katherine and Henry Carey were the children of Henry VIII, it is curious he did not acknowledge them as he had with Henry Fitzroy. Although a daughter was less significant, Henry, who was sensitive about his lack of heirs, would surely have admitted to being the father of Mary's son.[23]

One possible answer is that Henry was becoming emotionally involved with Anne Boleyn at the time the boy was born; to acknowledge a child by her sister would have caused outrage at court and in the wider Tudor society.

It is certainly true that Henry was extremely sensitive about the fact that, after sixteen years of marriage to Katherine of Aragon, he still had no legitimate male heir. As a result, it has been speculated that he found it 'safer to risk begetting children whose paternity could be denied than bastards who only emphasized his lack of legitimate heirs'.[24] This, of course, explains why he did not mind if his mistresses were married.

It is also worth noting that Henry had already decided to discard Queen Katherine and replace her with a new wife who would, he confidently expected, give him sons. Naturally, any sons Henry had with his new Queen would be the rightful heirs to the kingdom. Even if it was true, as has been speculated, that Henry was cultivating Henry Fitzroy to inherit his crown, he would, in this scenario, be no more than a useful stand-by, someone to be brought out in the event of a failure to produce a son or should that son die prematurely. In short, Henry simply had no need to acknowledge these children.

There are, then, arguments both for and against King Henry's being the father of Katherine and Henry Carey.

Against is the fact that Mary was married at the time of her relationship with Henry. There was nothing to say that the children could not have been her husband's. This is unarguable. Since Henry did not require exclusivity from his mistresses, Katherine and Henry Carey could indeed have been fathered by William Carey.

Other arguments are not so convincing. One is the fact that Henry did not acknowledge these children. This can be explained by his increasing involvement with Anne Boleyn. To acknowledge children born to him by her sister would have been inappropriate in the extreme. Also, due to his advancement of Henry Fitzroy, Henry had no need to acknowledge two more illegitimate children. Lastly, Henry was highly sensitive about having no legitimate male heir; to acknowledge Mary's children would merely have highlighted this difficult situation.

Another reason why Katherine and Henry Carey could be discounted as Henry's children is attributed to the King's low fertility. Again, this can be explained. There is nothing to suggest any physical cause; rather, Henry's problem was probably psychological, brought about by the pressure to produce a legitimate heir and the continuing anxiety over his failure to do so.

In the case of Henry Carey, that he was born after Mary's relationship with Henry had ended would seem to suggest that he, at least, was William Carey's son. However, although the relationship had undoubtedly come to an end at the time of his birth, it was still ongoing at the time of his conception, thus allowing for the possibility that Henry was the father.

What, then, of the evidence in favour of Katherine and Henry Carey being Henry's children? Again, it is circumstantial and open to debate. In the case of Katherine, she was certainly conceived and born while Mary Boleyn was Henry's mistress. Moreover, Katherine's friendship with Queen Elizabeth is strongly suggestive of a close family tie, perhaps even closer than that of cousin. Katherine's 'royal' and enormously expensive funeral is one manifestation of this.

In Henry Carey's case, the rumours and gossip surrounding him and contemporary speculation that he was the King's son, give us pause for thought. Like his sister, he, too, had a good relationship with Queen Elizabeth and he did well during her reign.

However, the most convincing arguments are the various grants and awards made to William Carey, and which coincide with the birth dates, albeit somewhat roughly in the case of Henry Carey, of the two children.

Naturally, each of these arguments, taken in isolation, cannot support claims that Henry VIII was the father of Katherine and Henry Carey. Taken together the case becomes much stronger. The evidence in support, although not exactly conclusive, does, on balance, outweigh the evidence against. As such, there is a high probability that Katherine and Henry Carey were the illegitimate children of Henry VIII.

1. Mary Boleyn: Usually overshadowed by her younger sister, Anne, Mary is a fascinating character in her own right.

2. Sir Thomas Boleyn: Mary's father depicted here in his robes as a Knight of the Garter. Mary could not compete with Anne in her father's affections.

3. (Opposite) Henry VIII: Mary's relationship with the King lasted over three years. Her love was unconditional and selfless. Strong evidence suggests that her two children were fathered by Henry.

4. Henry VIII processes to the opening of parliment, 4 February 1512.

5. Katherine of Aragon from a carving in Christchurch Priory.

6. William Carey: Mary's first husband was one of Henry's favourites. Athletic and intellectual, he enjoyed a steady career at court. He also looked the other way when Mary became Henry's mistress and benefited materially from the liaison.

7. Mary Tudor and Charles Brandon: Mary Tudor married Charles Brandon following the death of her first husband, King Louis XII of France. Her obvious manipulation of events possibly encouraged Mary who, in later years, married for love.

8. François I: The King of France knew Mary as a great prostitute, worse than the others. He had a brief affair with Mary before passing her on to his favourites.

9. Thomas Cromwell: Although a ruthless politician, this did not prevent him from assisting women who had been widowed or who had been abandoned by their families.

10. Katherine Knollys, née Carey: Mary's daughter, born during her relationship with Henry VIII, was probably the child of the King.

11. Henry Carey, Mary's son: Mary's relationship with King Henry was nearing its end as her second child was conceived. It is probable that the boy was Henry's.

12. & 13. Hever Castle, Kent: Inherited by Mary's father, Mary spent much of her childhood here.

14. Penshurst Place, Kent: Close to Hever, Penshurst Place was probably one of the houses used as a trysting place by Mary and King Henry.

15. Rochford Hall, Essex: This was the home of Mary and her second husband, William Stafford, following the downfall of her family.

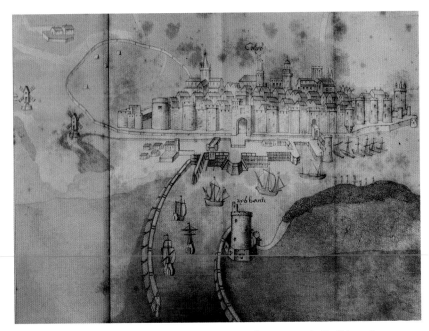

16. Calais: Mary travelled to Calais at least three times from Dover. As English territory at the time, Calais was garrisoned by English troops. Mary's second husband, William Stafford, was a soldier here.

17. Field of Cloth of Gold: Mary, newly married to William Carey, attended this meeting between King Henry and King François, which was a riot of colour, music and excitement.

18. Dancers: Life and the court of King Henry VIII was renowned for its pleasures and entertainments. Mary was a regular feature at pageants and dances, such as this one.

ANA BOLINA · ANG · RECIN

20. Blickling Hall, Norfolk: Almost certainly the birthplace of Mary Boleyn, Blickling had belonged to her family for several generations.

19. (Opposite) Anne Boleyn: Mary's younger sister who replaced her in the affections of King Henry, although this did not permanently damage relations between the two women.

21. Greenwich Palace by Anthony Van den Wyngaerde c.1544: Mary's husband, William Carey, was made keeper of the manor, garden and tower of Pleasance in Greenwich. It is possible that Henry and Mary used the palace as one of their trysting places.

22. York Place by Anthony Van den Wyngaerde c.1544: Now Whitehall Palace, York Place was refurbished by Henry VIII. Anne Boleyn and her family, including Mary, had apartments there.

CHAPTER 8

Out of Favour, 1526–1528

She wept and wrung her hands withal,

The tears fell in my neck:

She turned her face, and let it fall;

And scarce therewith could speak

As a gentleman of the privy chamber, William Carey had right of access to the King virtually twenty-four hours a day. The duties laid out in the Eltham Ordinances offer an insight into how the Careys passed their days.[1]

Anyone lodged at court was to have only the number of servants appropriate to their degree and station. Other servants could be kept, but they must be lodged in the town or outside the gates of the court. Servants were to go about their business for themselves and not engage 'lads and other rascals' to do their work for them. Also, they must be well behaved.

Mealtimes were strictly laid down. Dinner was served at ten in the morning on eating days; that is, on days other than fast days, while supper was served at four. On holidays, the first dinner would be served after the King had gone to chapel; likewise with supper. When the King's hall was not kept, dinner and supper times in both the King's and the Queen's chambers were eleven o'clock and six o'clock respectively. Meanwhile, no liveries of meat or drink would be served at any of the chambers of the court at the time of hall keeping except for those where such practice was customary and in the counting house. This last would concern Thomas Boleyn, who was Treasurer of the King's household between 1522 and 1525.

In order to prevent the devil making work of idle hands, the King decided he would keep hall continuously whenever he stayed at Windsor, Bewdley, Richmond, Hampton Court, Greenwich, Eltham or Woodstock. Chapel would also be kept at such times, making a fairly rigid routine.

No dogs, not even greyhounds, would be allowed at court except for a few small spaniels for the ladies. If the Careys kept dogs for hunting, they were to be kept in kennels outside. Moreover, if they went hunting, they first had to ensure that they obtained the necessary licences from the landowners. Meanwhile, fuel, lighting, bread and wine all came under regulation in order to prevent purloining in the King's houses and those of noblemen and gentlemen wherever the King might lodge. This was a regular occurrence, much to the dishonour of the King.

The King's chambers were to be kept 'pure and clean and free from great resort of people who disturb the king's retirement' by means of strictly controlling who was and who was not allowed to enter without the King's permission. Among those given free access were William Carey, gentleman, and his old friend, Henry Courtenay, Marquis of Exeter.

The gentlemen of the privy chamber were required to be ready at seven o'clock, or earlier if the King chose to rise early, in order to help him to dress. They were to help him put on his garments in a 'reverent, discreet, and sober manner'. The grooms or ushers were forbidden to touch the King's person without special command or to handle his garments except to warm them and carry them to the gentlemen who would then dress the King.

Every night two gentlemen were to lie on the pallet within the King's chamber. This was prepared each night by the grooms, who would also make up the fires according to orders before they returned to their lodgings.

'Immoderate' play of dice, cards or tables was not allowed in the privy chamber during the King's absence. However, 'moderate' play was allowed provided the players desisted when the King entered. No one should approach the King further than their station allowed. Also, the nearer they were to the King, the more humble they should show themselves.

When the King desired bread or drink, a gentlemen usher of the privy chamber commanded one of the grooms to warn the officers of the buttery, pantry and cellar to fetch it to the door of the privy chamber. Here an usher would collect it and place it on the cupboard until one of the six gentlemen, perhaps William Carey, should take it to the King.

The same procedure was followed at breakfast and when the King was served during the night. Mealtimes, however, were not rigidly fixed and the gentlemen shared their duties between the King and the chamber. Their own meals were to be taken in one mess at a convenient place assigned to them by the ushers.

The gentlemen would accompany the King to the hunt, on walks and at other sports. No one else would approach the King at these times unless he had appointed them and they had been warned beforehand by the gentlemen.

All this shows a rigid hierarchy among the servants of the King, who were governed by a strict regime. As a gentleman of the privy chamber, William Carey's duties gave him unrestricted access to King Henry. He tended him as he ate, dressed and even slept. He accompanied him to his sport and exercise and he conveyed orders to those whom the King wished to see. A list of those assigned accommodation in the King's house shows that William and Mary Carey were lodged close to the King. Therefore, although Mary was in service to Queen Katherine, she lived in the King's house with her husband rather than lodging with the Queen's ladies.

William Carey was certainly a man whose moment had arrived. He was basking in the King's favour. He held a secure post and he was in possession of several lucrative estates. To reflect his status, he had his portrait painted by the Flemish artist, Lucas Hornebolt. A copy was made much later and hung in the long gallery of Brooke House in Hackney. Known as the King's Palace at the time, this late-fifteenth-century manor would be extensively rebuilt by Mary's son, Henry Carey, when he became first Lord Hunsdon. The portrait shows Carey wearing cloth of gold, strikingly set off by the black and white of the rest of his costume.

It is possible that Hornebolt also painted a miniature portrait of Mary at this time.[2] This portrait is in classic Hornebolt style. One copy of it notes the sitter's age as twenty-five and was once believed to be an image of Anne Boleyn. Later it was said to be Jane Seymour on the strength that it had once belonged to Jane's brother, Edward, Duke of Somerset. However, the earliest member of the Seymour family to have owned this miniature is Charles Seymour, who lived from 1662 to 1748. Because of the sitter's resemblance to Anne Boleyn, it is possible that it is, in fact, Mary. The age of the sitter corresponds with the age Mary was in the mid-1520s, while the small show of hair beneath the gabled hood, the shade of her eyebrows and the colour of her eyes are consistent with the portrait of Mary previously described.

Mary Boleyn might have lost her place in the King's affections, but her brother, George, was continuing to make his way at court. In 1524, close to the time Mary gave birth to her daughter, he was given the manor of Grimston in Norfolk. About the same time he was received into the King's privy chamber.[3] This promotion might have been in response to a request from Mary, which the King was only too happy to grant in view of his satisfaction at the outcome of her pregnancy.

Although he had not survived the purge of the Eltham ordinances of 1526, this did not spoil the merits of George Boleyn. Later that year he was married to Jane Parker, a daughter of Henry Parker, tenth Baron Morley, a gentleman usher to the King. Through her mother, Alice, daughter of Sir John St John Bletsoe, Jane was related to King Henry's grandmother, the formidable Lady Margaret Beaufort, Countess of Richmond.

The marriage negotiations were probably initiated by the bride's father. For some time Lord Morley had been organising his affairs and in May 1523, his son and heir, Henry Morley, was married to Grace Newport. Shortly afterwards, he began his search for a suitable husband for his daughter.

The Boleyns were certainly worthy of Lord Morley's attention. Their success at court, their high favour with King Henry and their many estates which brought in substantial incomes ensured that they could not be ignored. Moreover, Sir Thomas had just added to his wealth by selling his estate of New Hall to King Henry for the magnificent sum of £1,000. To all this George was heir.

George had his personal attractions as well. He was probably about the same age as Jane. Although no portrait of him exists, he was said to have been good looking. Walpole, paraphrasing Antony Wood, notes that he was 'much adored at court, especially by the female sex, for his admirable discourse and symmetry of body; which one may well believe'.[4]

George was certainly accomplished. One of his interests was music. He was also known to have written poetry, a love he shared with his sister, Anne, and their friend, Thomas Wyatt. Sadly, very little remains of his literary endeavours; one song alone has survived and even its authorship is disputed. George was especially interested in theology which was for him no casual intellectual pursuit.

Events were taking a new turn in King Henry's relationship with Anne Boleyn as well. At a court ball held in honour of the French ambassadors on 5 May 1527 Anne is mentioned among the guests. That Mary's name does not appear is not necessarily significant; the Venetian ambassadors note only the presence of some 200 'damsels'.[5]

The main purpose of the occasion was to show off the Princess Mary to the ambassadors, who had come to continue negotiations for a marriage between her and either François I or his second son, Henry, Duc d'Orléans. It was she who took centre stage. However, the King chose Anne as his dancing partner and this was, in fact, her first public appearance with Henry.

During the summer of 1527 Henry's court progress stopped at Beaulieu for the unusually long period of one month. There was a reason. Accompanying the King were the Dukes of Norfolk and Suffolk, the Marquis of Exeter, Viscount Fitzwalter and the Earls of Rutland, Oxford and Essex. Also present was Sir Thomas Boleyn, Viscount Rochford who, with the Duke of Norfolk, represented Anne's family. On the agenda was Henry's divorce from Queen Katherine, or perhaps more accurately, his remarriage to Anne. The outcome was the application to the Pope for the annulment of Henry's marriage. While the application made it clear that the King intended to remarry and beget a legitimate heir, it did not reveal the name of the lady he had chosen.

The grounds for the annulment were that Henry and Katherine were related in the first degree of affinity. That is, Henry believed that his marriage to Katherine was invalid because she had been married to his brother, Arthur. This meant that, as it was understood at the time, Katherine was Henry's sister. She was, therefore, out of bounds as a wife. However, the fifteen-year-old Arthur had died after only a few months of marriage and there were doubts over whether or not the marriage had been consummated. The dispensation granted at the time had taken this uncertainty into consideration and documents were produced to allow Henry and Katherine to marry whatever the circumstances.

Now Henry wanted the Pope to revise his dispensation to allow him to take a new wife even though his marriage to Katherine had not yet been annulled. In fact, the annulment of marriages was fairly common and Popes were generally accommodating wherever possible, especially with princes. Even Henry's brother-in-law, Charles Brandon, Duke of Suffolk, had managed to obtain permission to annul his first marriage to Margaret Mortimer on the grounds of consanguinity. He had subsequently remarried, more than once as it happened. His example shows that Henry was confident of being granted the dissolution of his own marriage to Katherine and that acquiring the necessary documentation would be a mere formality.

On the other hand, what Henry was really asking the Pope for was a dispensation that would technically allow him to commit bigamy. This was very far from being a mere formality. It was only when Cardinal Wolsey, who had been kept in the dark concerning this particular request, heard about it that Henry decided to abandon it.

A second bull was issued. This time, and again without Wolsey's knowledge, Henry's asked for permission, in the event of an annulment, to marry a woman to whom he was related in the first degree of affinity due to previous illicit sexual relations.[6] Here, then, Henry's relationship with Mary had become an impediment to his intended marriage to Anne. Technically, such a relationship could not be dispensed with; however, as we have seen, Popes were frequently willing to bend the rules. Henry was confident that the Pope would be accommodating as he sought another special dispensation.

In the estimation of his cousin, Reginald Pole, Henry's hypocrisy in this matter knew no bounds. Henry wanted to divorce one wife on the grounds of her previous relationship with his brother. Now he was seeking to marry a second wife, even though he was related to her in much the same way. Pole pointed this out to Henry at a later date in a work known as *Pro ecclesiasticae unitatis defensione*, or *In Defence of the Unity of the Church*, which took the form of a letter. He accused the King of being motivated by passion not conscience:

> [God] has shown it through the very person whom you have chosen
> to fill the place of your lawful wife. For who is she? The sister of
> a woman, whom you had long kept as a mistress. But did you not
> know that the law, which forbids you to marry the relict of your

brother, if he had known her carnally, also forbids you to marry
the woman, whose sister you have carnally known yourself?[7]

As noted, this book was written at a much later date; to be precise,
Pole began work on it in the summer of 1536, a few weeks after
Anne Boleyn's execution. In all fairness to Henry, at this earlier
stage of the long journey towards making Anne his wife and
Queen, he was thinking in a more subtle way than is allowed
for in Pole's rebuke. Henry's approach was influenced by a literal
reading of Leviticus 20.21. Here, it is stated that 'If a man takes
his brother's wife, it is impurity; he has uncovered his brother's
nakedness, they shall be childless.' Henry justified the legality of
his intended marriage to Anne on the grounds that she had not
been his brother's wife but simply the sister of a former mistress.[8]

The Pope had different ideas. He interpreted the Leviticus
passage as being inapplicable to Henry's situation because it
referred to a brother's wife, not his widow. That is, it concerned
adultery and not affinity. Furthermore, the Pope's view found
confirmation in Deuteronomy 25.5, in which a man is actually
instructed to marry his brother's widow if the marriage had
produced no sons, thus providing a surrogate heir for his dead
brother.[9] Henry stubbornly, or in desperation, refused to revise
his own understanding of Leviticus 20.21. As far as he was
concerned the Pope had been wrong to issue the dispensation
allowing him to marry Katherine. The marriage was null and
void as a consequence, and Henry wanted this to be admitted.
He was troubled by the technical difficulties surrounding the

issuing of the first dispensation. Only later did he come to understand, or to admit, that such relationships were opposed by divine law and could not be dispensed with.[10]

Now, while the rest of her family were in the ascendant, Mary was left on the sidelines. Once Henry had discarded her, she returned to her life with William Carey. Her son, whom she named Henry, was born on 4 March 1526 and it seems that she accepted her lot. Other women might not have found the transition from King's mistress to an ordinary member of the household of the Queen she had wronged so palatable. This would be all the more so if, like Mary, she had been set aside in favour of her sister.

Mary remained silent about her feelings when she saw the man she had loved become involved with her own sister. It is possible, although improbable, that the relationship had come to a natural end even before Henry's eye had fallen on Anne and that Mary had stepped aside with indifference. Even so, it would not have been unnatural had Mary felt at least a twinge of jealousy. After all, her relationship with Henry had been lengthy; she had been the centre of his world and the object of his love for more than three years, a significant period of time. There must have been residual feelings.

Perhaps Mary had become Henry's mistress with the sole intention of gaining favours and advancement for her family. If so, she had been quite successful. Both her husband – and especially her father – had benefited from her liaison with the King. Had this been the case, her setting aside would not have been such an emotional wrench, although there would probably have been more than a little hurt pride. On the other hand, it is more acceptable to believe, and as her future behaviour will support, that Mary had simply fallen in love with Henry and, following the dictates of her heart rather than her head, she had become his mistress and abandoned herself to the delights of a love affair with he who was, at the time, the most desirable prince in Christendom.

As far as is known, Mary never asked for anything for herself from Henry. The difficult circumstances she faced subsequent to her being put aside would seem to support the supposition that she made no material gain from their relationship. Could Mary have been so selfless that she would step aside so easily and so readily without even a show of protest when she saw that Henry's attention had strayed, even when she saw that the new object of Henry's attention was her own sister? Is it possible that Mary, far from accepting her situation, chose instead to exact revenge on her sister? If so, she was well placed to do so.

Anne's relationship with Henry had a divisive effect on the court. People were split between supporters of Katherine, who are usually referred to as the 'Aragonese faction', and those who followed Anne. The Aragonese faction was particularly powerful. Its main point of contact with the Queen was Margaret Pole, Countess of Salisbury. Margaret was the daughter of George, Duke of Clarence, who had been executed by his own brother for treason in 1478. Her son, the aforementioned Reginald Pole, at first seemed indifferent towards Henry's divorce and was even given the assignment of securing the favourable opinion of the university doctors of Paris on the King's behalf. He would later claim, unconvincingly, to have tried to avoid this task. Another son, Henry Pole, Lord Montague, had married Jane, daughter of George Neville, third Baron Bergavenny, which brought him into the sphere of Edward Stafford, Duke of Buckingham, who was Bergavenny's father-in-law. The influence of the White Rose cannot be mistaken in all this. Margaret Pole was also cousin to Henry Courtenay. Courtenay married, as his second wife, Gertrude Blount, daughter of William Blount, Lord Mountjoy, chamberlain to Queen Katherine.

The power of this tightly-knit faction waned somewhat after 1514 as Wolsey's star rose, but it soon recovered. However, it experienced a major blow in 1521 when Buckingham was executed. Again, it recovered. Margaret was appointed governess to Princess Mary, while Courtenay was created Marquis of Exeter and appointed as one of only two noblemen serving in the privy chamber.

As Anne Boleyn's power increased to the point where she posed a threat to Katherine, the Aragonese faction was well placed to offer the Queen powerful support. They were to remain loyal to Katherine even when all was lost. Exeter's name appears alongside that of Montague among the peers who condemned Anne Boleyn to death.

As we have seen, Exeter was a royal favourite and it was probably he who had introduced William Carey to court.

Carey likewise became intimate with the King and it is possible that Henry had arranged his marriage to Mary Boleyn. As Henry's involvement with Anne grew more serious, Carey might have had a difficult choice to make. Would he remain loyal to his friend, Exeter, and to the King to whom he owed so much, or would he side with his wife's family, the Boleyns, and support them as they followed a course that would place their second daughter on the throne.

Certainly Anne knew that she needed all the help she could get. There were really only three people to whom she could turn for support. The first was her father, Sir Thomas. Although his rewards had stopped when Mary's relationship with Henry ended, he was still in favour with the King due, in part, to the ascendancy of Anne. The same could be said of Anne's second pillar of support, her brother, George, even though he had not survived Wolsey's pruning of the King's household under the Eltham Ordinances. Anne's third supporter was Thomas Wyatt, a former admirer newly arrived back at court after a diplomatic mission to Italy. There was also, of course, Henry Percy, now sixth Earl of Northumberland, but he preferred to remain on his estates far from the court. Anne, then, turned to her brother-in-law, William Carey. In an attempt to win him over, she offered to assist him as he sought to secure the appointment of his sister, Eleanor, as abbess at the nunnery of St Edith following the death of the previous incumbent.

Had William Carey joined Exeter against Anne Boleyn, Mary would have been faced with a stark choice indeed. She could defy her husband and side with her family; alternatively, she could turn her back on the Boleyns and join the Aragonese faction in support of Queen Katherine. As it turned out, she would be spared this difficulty, although for the unhappiest of reasons. During the summer of 1528 an epidemic of sweating sickness broke out and it turned Mary's world upside down.

The sweating sickness is believed to have made its first appearance in England during the autumn of 1485. Many thought that it had been brought to the country by the Breton and French mercenaries who had assisted Henry Tudor to overthrow Richard III. Given that the disease appeared only in Calais, which was English territory at the time, and that France had not been affected, this seems improbable. More plausible is that it arrived via the ports of Yorkshire and Lincolnshire on trading ships from Scandinavia and Russia.

The disease was described as 'new', indicating that the symptoms were very different to those of known illnesses, such as the plague. The onset was sudden, the Tudor chronicler, Holinshed,[11] notes that the 'malady was so cruel that it killed some within three hours, some within two hours, some merry at dinner and dead at supper'. Victims would become feverish with terrible headaches, muscular pain especially affecting the back, limbs and abdomen, rapid heartbeat and the characteristic profuse sweating.[12]

Although it is now understood that the sweat was a viral infection transmitted to humans by rats, sixteenth-century doctors had no idea what caused the disease. German physicians were particularly interested in it since its spread to their lands. Then there was a general preoccupation with English affairs as a result of altercations between Henry VIII and Luther and the emerging proto-Protestantism in England. Perhaps inspired by this, Hermann von Neuenahr speculated that the illness was attributable to divine retribution. Johann Wier disagreed. Looking for a scientific explanation, he pointed out that the climate of Britain was fairly constant, whereas the disease appeared only periodically. Taking a similar approach, Johann Volg suggested that the air of Britain had a 'hidden mysterious quality', which gave it an unnatural character from time to time.[13]

Ignorance of the cause of the sweat meant that treatment was little more than experimental; one doctor recommended wrapping the patient in warm clothes and giving him beer to drink.[14] Many agreed that keeping the patient warm was the best remedy, the idea being that the perspiration would somehow carry away whatever it was that had caused the illness. Victims taken ill during the day were told to go to bed fully clothed and remain there for twenty-four hours. Those struck down during the night were not to get up but to remain in bed, again for twenty-four hours. The timing is significant: the sweat took its victims swiftly; anyone who was still alive after twenty-four hours was usually safe.

As soon as the sweat appeared, the court was immediately broken up. Henry withdrew to Waltham while Anne returned to Hever Castle with her father. Henry, terrified of any illness, kept as few servants with him as possible. He wrote to Cardinal Wolsey with advice on how to avoid becoming ill: 'use small suppers, drink little wine, "namely, that is big", and once in the week use pills of Rasis; and if it come, to sweat moderately, and at the full time, without suffering it to run in'.[15] As it was, Wolsey became ill, but he survived.

Then Anne Boleyn caught the illness, as did her father. Henry wanted to send his chief physician, Dr Chambers, but he was not available and Dr Butts was sent instead. His prognosis was not good on account of the 'turning in of the sweat before the time'.[16] George likewise became ill, which was particularly frightening for Henry since George had accompanied the King to Waltham. His symptoms developed soon after arriving at the house.

Still, Henry's strategy of quarantining himself paid off and he survived. Others were not so lucky. The man to whom Henry had entrusted the delicate task of helping him procure ladies, Sir William Compton, was struck down and died within a few hours. Henry moved on to Hunsdon and, just as he was going to bed, was given the news that William Carey had died. It was 22 June 1528; Mary Boleyn was a widow.[17]

Mary was now in a very difficult situation. The loss of her husband was bad enough, but she also had two very young children to look after. What was worse, her father had turned his back on her. Now that Mary had been discarded by the King she was no longer the source of advancement she had once been and she lost her place of importance within the family. Sir Thomas appears to have made no attempt to help his daughter sort out the legal work that was necessary in her situation. As such, her jointure went unpaid and, although Mary continued to hold the manor of Traceys after Carey's death, the revenues were not enough to sustain her. Abandoned and in desperation, Mary appealed to the only person she believed would help her: King Henry.

Henry, it is clear, still felt some affection for his former mistress, the mother of two of his children, and this translated into genuine concern for her plight. He took it upon himself to assist her, intervening with her father on her behalf. Indeed, it took direct action from the King to prompt Sir Thomas to make provision for Mary and her children. As he wrote to Anne, Mary was in 'extreme necessity', adding that it was their father's duty to support her:

> As touching your sister's matter, I have caused Walter Welze to write to my Lord [Viscount Rochford] my mind therein, whereby I trust that Eve shall not have power to deceive Adam; for surely, whatsoever is said, it cannot so stand with his honour but that he must needs take her his natural daughter now in her extreme necessity.[18]

The phrase, her 'extreme necessity' has spawned speculation that Mary might have been carrying a child by another man at the time of William Carey's death.[19] There is nothing to support this idle speculation. Mary's predicament was more than enough to justify the phrase.

Henry's phrase 'Eve shall not have power to deceive Adam' is difficult. Since it clearly refers to temptation, it is possible that Henry referred Mary's case to her father so that he would not be tempted by her womanly tears to act inappropriately.

Henry's assistance did not end there. Shortly afterwards, he granted the wardship and marriage of Henry Carey to Anne, who also had the custody of William Carey's lands during the boy's minority.[20] In fact, while this relieved Mary from the burden of providing for her son, it also benefited Anne. Because property passed to children, not to widows, Henry Carey's wardship gave Anne the revenues of his estates.

Anne, in her turn, provided an excellent education for the boy. He was taught by Nicolas Bourbon, a French scholar exiled for his evangelical beliefs and given refuge in England by Anne. He taught his pupils the principles of reform, no doubt to the great satisfaction of his patroness. Henry Carey was educated alongside other royal wards, such as Henry Norris, the son of the courtier of the same name, and Thomas Hervey.

Anne provided her assistance to Mary in another matter as well. By the time of his death William Carey's attempt to secure the appointment of his sister, Eleanor, as abbess of Wilton was still ongoing. Anne continued to offer her support to the cause as a kindness to her sister. Henry assured her that he would agree to the appointment provided Eleanor's credentials were satisfactory. Upon investigation, however, Wolsey discovered that Eleanor Carey had borne two children by two priests and that she had later become the mistress of Lord Broke, a layman. 'Wherefore,' Henry wrote to his beloved, 'I would not, for all the gold in the world, clog your conscience nor mine to make her ruler of a house, which is of so ungodly demeanour; nor, I trust, you would not that neither for brother nor sister I should so distain mine honour of conscience.' Eleanor's elder sister, also a nun at Wilton, was also deemed unsuited to the post due to a dubious reputation.[21] Wolsey promoted his own candidate, Dame Isabelle Jordan, who was prioress at the abbey and the preferred choice of the nuns, but Henry was forced to reject even her on account of her age and doubtful reputation.[22]

Anne was unable to help Mary in this instance, but her influence over the King was such that she began to secure benefits for other members of her family. Therefore, on 26 September, George Boleyn was appointed squire of the body and was awarded an annuity of fifty marks, payable by the chief butler of England from the issues of the prizes of wines.

Towards the end of the year, Mary's financial situation was eased somewhat when she was awarded an annuity of £100, previously granted by the King to William Carey.[23]

This annuity enabled Mary to face the New Year celebrations in a more secure situation financially, but it was to be a lonely festive season. Her husband was dead, her sister had taken her place in the King's affections and, although she was now living under her father's roof, it was clear that he had little love for her. Mary's world had become a cold and friendless place indeed.

CHAPTER 9

Mary Eclipsed, 1529–1532

Noli me tangere; for Caesar's I am,

And wild for to hold, though I seem tame

The fortunes of the Boleyns, rising as they had been for some time, positively soared during 1529. Except for Mary, that is. On 1 February of that year George was made chief steward of Beaulieu, or New Hall, for which he would receive 10*l* a year, and keeper of the New Park with 3d a day.[1] These grants had previously been held by Mary's late husband, William Carey.

Although the age of George Boleyn is not known, when he was appointed to a diplomatic mission in France in October, the French ambassador, Jean du Bellay, considered him to be too young for the post.[2] This did not seem to have deterred Henry, whose generosity towards the Boleyns was great indeed. The newly-knighted George was duly sent on his way.

There were more honours to come. On 8 December, George was created Viscount Rochford while his father, Sir Thomas, became Earl of Wiltshire and Ormond.[3] The following day a banquet was given at court to celebrate the good fortune of the Boleyns. To the Imperial ambassador, Eustache Chapuys, the occasion resembled nothing more than a wedding feast. He was astounded to see Anne sitting at the King's side, a place properly reserved for the Queen.[4]

It was now abundantly clear to anyone who might yet be unconvinced that Anne was intended to take Katherine's place as the new Queen of England. Chapuys, a fervent champion of Katherine of Aragon, found this scene distasteful, which makes it all the more surprising that he actually referred to Anne as 'the Lady Anne', rather than his usual 'the Lady' or 'the Concubine'. Although Mary Boleyn was probably present at this banquet, Chapuys does not mention her. Perhaps the ambassador, who had come to court only four months previously, was not fully acquainted with the various members of the Boleyn family. More probable is that he simply did not notice her. Mary had been entirely eclipsed by Anne.

One thing that is very clear, though, is Chapuys's belief that the Earl of Wiltshire's elevation had been due solely to Anne's favour with the King. This must, of course, have been part of it. Sir Thomas had certainly benefited from the favour shown to both his daughters by the King as well as his own willingness to look the other way. On the other hand, he was a very capable man in his own right and, even without the parts played by Mary and Anne in the King's affections, he was talented enough to advance at court, although, perhaps, not so high.

If Mary had not been aware of Anne's new position with Henry by now, it became all too clear to her in November 1530, when Henry gave Anne £20 to redeem a jewel from her.[5] This jewel had possibly been given to Mary in payment of a gambling debt; equally possible is that Henry had given it to her as a love token. All memory of Mary's place in Henry's heart had to be erased, it seems.

Watching as she was from the margins, neither belonging nor banished, Mary had a unique perspective on the events that unfolded as a result of her former lover's attempts to replace Katherine with Anne. When Henry had requested a papal dispensation to marry Anne in 1527, the couple thought it would be an easy thing to grant and that they would be married within a few months. Now, four years later, Anne and Henry were still striving to make their hopes a reality. One obstacle was the Pope's doubts concerning Henry's argument. This stemmed, as we know, from the King's rigid interpretation of Leviticus 20.21 and, by extension, his conviction that Pope Julius II had overstepped his authority in granting the dispensation which had allowed Henry to marry Katherine of Aragon.

Another problem had been the rise of Charles V. The Emperor was Katherine's nephew, and his military successes at Pavia in 1525 and at Rome two years later gave him dominance in Italy. The Pope had been forced to flee to the Castel Sant'Angelo and was in no position to assist Henry as he sought to dissolve his marriage with Charles's aunt. Walking a fine line, he did all he could to give the appearance of trying to help Henry while working in the background to delay matters for as long as possible. In the end, however, he did grant permission for Henry to remarry, but it was on condition that Henry could prove that his marriage to Katherine had been unlawful.

Queen Katherine, who was initially kept in the dark concerning the investigation into her marriage, did not remain so for long. She contacted Charles V and the Pope with what was to be the main thrust of her defence. This was that her marriage to Prince Arthur had not been consummated and, therefore, had never really existed. She had been a virgin when she married Henry.

With battle lines drawn, it became a matter of some importance where the case for annulment would be tried. Katherine knew she would have a fair hearing only if it went to Rome. Henry also knew this and so he requested, and was granted, a legatine commission to empower Wolsey and Cardinal Lorenzo Campeggio to hear the case in England.

Cardinal Campeggio was Cardinal Protector of England and Bishop of Salisbury. He was also crippled with gout and it took him several weeks to make the journey to England. Still, he managed and, after he had rested a while, the case got underway. A legatine court was finally opened in June. Katherine first appealed to Rome and then she turned to Henry, urging him to admit that she had been a virgin when she married him. Henry would do no such thing. The Queen walked out of court never to return. The court dragged on until the end of July, when Campeggio announced an adjournment until October.

The court reconvened in October but no progress was made. Anne Boleyn confided to the King her belief that

Wolsey was deliberately delaying the proceedings with the result that Henry lost confidence in the cardinal. This marked the beginning of Wolsey's downfall. His fate was sealed when he advised Henry against an alliance with France, an alliance Henry himself had proposed as a critical step if the impasse over the marriage were to be broken. Wolsey's enemies, specifically Norfolk, Suffolk and Anne's father, Wiltshire, urged the King to charge him with *praemunire*; that is of resorting to the jurisdiction of a higher authority, in this case the Pope, over that of the King. Wolsey pleaded guilty and was stripped of his offices except that of Archbishop of York.

Even so, the Boleyns and their allies recognised that Wolsey's power was such that he should not be left alone to live in peaceful retirement. They badgered him mercilessly, increasing their attacks when Henry began to show signs that he regretted having banished the cardinal. Rumours began to spread that Wolsey had entered into secret negotiations with both the Emperor Charles and François I. He was also said to have approached the Pope to request an order that Henry should put away Anne and take back Katherine. Such rumours might have been true, or they might have been the work of Wolsey's enemies; whichever way, when they were corroborated with reports from Bologna that a papal brief was to be issued in which Henry would be ordered to send Anne from court, Wolsey was held responsible.

Yet, it was French fears that England was about to enter into a *rapprochement* with Charles V that finally led to

Wolsey's ruin. These fears had been mysteriously revealed to Henry who finally understood how deeply Wolsey had been involved in foreign dealings. This was more than *praemunire*, it was treason. Wolsey was arrested by the Earl of Northumberland, Anne's former suitor, but the former cardinal's death at Leicester from natural causes in November 1530 ensured that he would cheat the headsman. Wolsey's death also freed the newly-reformed conciliar government to continue, as best it could, to work for Henry's annulment.

Meanwhile, Mary's family continued to reap the rewards of royal beneficence. In January 1530 her father was elevated to the Privy Council, having been made Lord Privy Seal. However, relations between Henry and Anne were far from tranquil. They had argued. Henry had reproached Anne for having made him so many enemies. There was a tangible tension in the air. Henry was wise enough to realise that it was largely due to the incessant delays in their marriage plans. Another cause, he recognised, was the fact that Katherine was still living at court and was continuing to communicate with him, by letter or in person, as she had done throughout their married life. She also continued to make his shirts, a wifely duty she saw no reason to give up. All this both piqued and worried Anne. Henry's solution was to move Anne and her family into new lodgings. The place he chose for them was York Place.

Formerly the residence of Cardinal Wolsey as Archbishop of York, Henry had taken over York Place, where he continued the cardinal's massive building programme. The name was changed to Whitehall Palace, probably following the custom that any festival hall was referred to as a 'white hall', and the garden and orchard were laid out. Land was purchased in order to make room for the inevitable sporting facilities, including a tiltyard and tennis courts, even a cockpit, but also, perhaps, a bowing green.

Ambassador Chapuys noted that Anne felt at ease at York Place because, at the time, it had no separate state apartments for the Queen. Here, Anne could have Henry all to herself. Anne and her mother lodged in rooms beneath Wolsey's library. Sir Thomas and Lady Elizabeth also had rooms in the palace as did George and his wife, Jane. Although no mention is made of Mary, she is known to have resided at York Place, perhaps sharing accommodation with her sister and mother. Her annuity of £100 would certainly have allowed her to maintain some presence at court, where much of the money would be used to keep her in a style befitting the sister of the favourite.

Still, for both Mary Boleyn and Katherine of Aragon, the future looked far from being happy. Not long after the Boleyns moved into the sumptuous accommodation at York Place, Henry finally separated from his once much-beloved wife. Mary must have felt a certain empathy with the Queen, who, like herself, now lived outside the sphere of those she loved. Mary, while still living at court, seemed, nevertheless, to have been kept at arms length. Close at hand, but not belonging, the unwanted and unloved daughter, the discarded mistress; life was forlorn indeed. Katherine, on the other hand, had been forced to move out completely. Separated even from her daughter, the Princess Mary, she established a lonely household at the More.

While Mary had been Henry's mistress her relationship with him had never threatened Katherine. Mary had never attempted to take Henry away from her or to take her place as Queen. Indeed, such a thought would have been inconceivable. What had happened in those few intervening years must have astonished Mary. Even so, there were yet more surprises to come. Henry ruthlessly broke cherished traditions, destroyed the established order and saw those who had been his staunchest supporters go to their deaths, and all for the love of Mary's sister, the Lady Anne.

In 1530, Edward Fox, a former secretary to Cardinal Wolsey, was huddled with a team of scholars over various texts – biblical and early Christian as well as ancient English. These came to be known collectively as the *Collectania satis copiosa*. They were used to support the somewhat specious argument that the Anglo-Saxon Kings of England had been supreme in spiritual as well as temporal matters. These findings struck a chord with Henry, not least because they resonated with a book Anne had shown him some time previously. This book, *The Obedience of a Christian Man and How Christian Rulers Ought to Govern* by William Tyndale, asserted that the King was answerable to God alone and it was the duty of his subjects to obey him absolutely by commandment of God.

As Mary knew, Tyndale's views, as well as the findings of Fox and his team, ran counter to Henry's own beliefs. In his own work, *Assertio Septum Sacramentorum*, a polemic against Luther's anti-papal *De captivitate Babylonica*, Henry had condemned schism and upheld papal authority. So pleased was the Pope with the King's stance that he bestowed upon him the title 'Defender of the Faith'.

Now Henry's own beliefs were being challenged. His faith in the authority of the Pope was shaken by his conviction that Julius II had been mistaken in granting him a dispensation to marry his dead brother's wife. His subsequent support of the Pope had not secured him his wish to annul his first marriage and had done nothing to bring his second any closer. Perhaps it was time to follow in the footsteps of his Anglo-Saxon predecessors and assume royal supremacy in matters spiritual as well as temporal.

Henry VIII, then, set about making himself Head of the Church in England. It would not be an easy process. The clergy appealed to the oath they made to the Pope at their ordination. They gave in to the King's demands only after being charged with *praemunire*, for which they had been pardoned in exchange for a fee of £100,000. Cowed, they accepted of the King as Supreme Head on earth of the Church in England. This title was mitigated somewhat by the caveat, 'as far as the law of Christ allows', although even that would, in time, be dropped. The case for the annulment of Henry's marriage to Katherine could now safely be tried in England. Soon he would be able to marry Anne, and his longed-for sons would follow.

Yet, for all that, Henry hesitated. He still entertained doubts about the validity of his marriage to Anne. If he married her while Katherine was still alive, there was every chance that he would face fierce opposition from his own aristocracy, from Charles V, from Rome. Perhaps, however, his worst fear was breaking with the religious principles and practices that he had known all his life. Now, as Head of the Church in England, Henry was entering into uncharted territory. His love for Anne was a guiding light, but he needed more. François I had offered Henry his support; now Henry felt the need to visit his brother monarch and to discuss the matter face-to-face. Arrangements were set in train for a meeting at Calais.

Of course, Anne Boleyn was to be the star at Calais but she could not go as plain Lady Anne. She expected to be received by the Queen of France and François's sister, Marguerite, now Queen of Navarre, and she needed a more exalted status. Henry, therefore, created Anne Marquis of Pembroke in her own right on 1 September 1532 in a magnificent ceremony. This was a masculine title and it was of great significance in the Tudor dynasty. Henry's father, Henry VII, was born at Pembroke Castle, while his great-uncle, Jasper Tudor, who had died when Henry was only four, had been Earl of Pembroke. The falcon was ready to soar.

CHAPTER 10

The Queen's Sister, 1532–1534

In court to serve decked with fresh array,

Of sugar'd meats feeling the sweet repast,

The life in banquets and sundry kinds of play

Amid the press of worldly looks to waste,

Hath with it join'd ofttimes such bitter taste,

That whoso joys such kind of life to hold,

In prison joys fetter'd with chains of gold

At five in the morning of Friday 11 October 1532 Mary Boleyn found herself standing once more on the dock at Dover. It was still dark and the cold breezes coming in from the Channel nipped her cheeks and caught her breath. All about her there was bustle. Men were loading ships with cargo and horses, huge boxes filled with sumptuous clothes, tapestries, furniture and gifts. Mary's own baggage was loaded along with that of her companions.

Mary looked at the King's ship, the *Swallow*, which was to take them to Calais. She thought about a time eighteen years previously when she stood on this very spot awaiting the change in the weather that would allow her to leave England for the first time. Then she had been in the entourage of

Mary Tudor, the King's sister.

The slow voyage across the dark and dangerous waters of the Channel allowed Mary time to reflect on how her life had changed since that time. She recalled the meeting of the two Kings at the Field of Cloth of Gold. She had been newly married to William Carey and was carried away with the exhilaration of life at court as the wife of one of Henry's own favourites. Not long after that Henry had 'noticed' her, as the saying went, and she became his mistress. This time Mary had not been passed on as soon as the King tired of her. She and Henry had shared a genuine love. It had produced two children. Mary was the only mistress Henry had not put aside as soon as she became pregnant; rather, he had continued to care for her and, when her daughter was born, Henry had taken her back. The relationship had come to a natural end not long after Mary's son was conceived. Yet, as with many relationships built upon mutual love and respect, Henry had retained some affection for Mary. Loneliness came into her life not with the loss of William Carey but with the loss of Henry, for that was when her family cast her out.

Thomas Boleyn, now pre-occupied with Anne, had no further interest in the daughter whose favour with the King had brought him handsome dividends. Henry had shown his affection once more when he helped Mary out of her difficult financial situation. Her father had been ordered to take her in. This, as well as her former relationship with Henry and its consequences, had put a strain on her relationship with her family. Ironically, it had been Anne who had taken pity on her. For at this point, it does seem as though Mary belonged to Anne's entourage as a maid of honour.

Now Mary was accompanying Anne to France. This visit promised to be every bit as lavish and exciting as the others. This time, however, the business of the two Kings had great significance for Mary's family and for her personally. The outcome of the voyage would pave the way for Anne to become Henry's new wife and Queen; Mary would become the Queen's sister. For this was what King Henry and Anne had long anticipated. They were going to meet King François who had offered his support for their impending marriage. It was a quirk of fate that could not have been lost on Mary. Anne's future happiness and the greatest achievement of the Boleyns rested upon the actions of two of Mary's former lovers. It was a strange situation indeed.

Having landed safely at Calais, Henry set out to meet François at Sandingfield. Here, Henry met for the first time François's sons, the Dauphin and the Dukes of Orléans and Angoulême, a poignant moment considering his own lack of heirs. The Kings then dined together before Henry returned to Calais to prepare for a return visit by François. The King of France was received with salvoes of artillery, the number of which greatly exceeded that of the welcome given to Henry.

François was treated to all manner of entertainments, including the obligatory jousts, but the real treat was yet to come:

> After supper a masque was held, in which danced Anne Boleyn,
> now Marchioness [*sic*] of Pembroke, Lady Mary Boleyn, Lady
> Derby, Lady Fitzwalter, Lady Rochford, Lady Lisle and Lady
> Wallop, all with visors on their faces and dressed in cloth of gold
> trimmed with crimson tinsel satin with waves of cloth of silver and
> tied with laces of gold. The ladies were brought into the chamber
> by four demoiselles dressed in crimson satin with tabards of fine
> Cyprus [thread] and they took the French King and other lords of
> France by the hand and danced a dance or two.[1]

François pretended to be suitably surprised when the ladies' visors were removed and he saw that his dancing partner was none other than the Lady Anne. The name of Mary's partner is not recorded; all that can be said was that he was a man of consequence, since all the men who danced with the ladies were lords of France.

Despite the great ceremony, the entertainments and the splendid gifts, the serious purpose of the meeting was not forgotten. The two Kings talked in private for some while. Matters discussed included the new Anglo-French *rapprochement* and the sending of two cardinals to Rome to announce it to the Pope. Also discussed was the conclusion of a marriage alliance between François's second son, Henri, to the Pope's niece, Catherine de' Medici.

The meeting had undoubtedly been a success. However, its main object, if the rumours were to be believed, remained uncertain. It had been speculated that Henry and Anne would marry while at Calais, but this was almost certainly not the case. Nevertheless, as they waited at Calais for the autumn fogs to clear, they felt secure enough in the success of the past few days that they did, finally, consummate their relationship.

After six years of keeping him at bay, Anne was now Henry's lover, but not in the way Mary had been. For Mary was never to be anything more than the King's mistress. With Anne it was entirely different. Anne was to be his new wife and his new Queen; she would have it no other way and Henry agreed to take her on her own terms.

At Christmas 1532 all went on as normal. Dancing, music and the exchange of gifts all took place in much the same way as they did in any other year. Mary is listed among the several ladies to receive New Year's gifts: gilt cruses, cups, salts, a lee pot, casting bottles and goblets. In return she gave the King a shirt with a collar of black lacework which she might have made herself.[2]

However, this was no ordinary Christmas. Already preparations were being made for Anne's wedding to Henry. The couple were married in a secret ceremony, with only a handful of witnesses on or about 25 January 1533. Ambassador Chapuys noted that Anne's parents, Sir Thomas and Lady Elizabeth, had attended, as had her brother, George. Chapuys also mentioned two favourites, but did not name them. It can be speculated, but no more, that they were Mary and her sister-in-law, Jane, Lady Rochford.

Whoever they were, the eagle-eyed among them might have noticed that Anne had another secret. She was pregnant.

Henry was now, technically, a bigamist and it became imperative to dissolve his marriage to Katherine as soon as may be, but there was another reason for such urgency. The validity of Henry's marriage to Anne must be accepted beyond all doubt in order to ensure the legitimacy of the child Anne was carrying. With the stakes raised, no effort was spared.

The Boleyn cause was greatly assisted by the death, the previous year, of William Warham, Archbishop of Canterbury. The one chosen to fill the vacancy for archbishop was Thomas Cranmer, who had been associated with the Boleyn family since at least 1529. At the time of his appointment he was in Italy in the train of Charles V. He had also recently married. His bride was related to the wife of the pastor of Nuremberg, Andreas Osiander, whom he had befriended while on a diplomatic mission. Cramner returned to England, keeping his marriage a secret, as he set about fulfilling the King's dearest wish.

The first task was to establish Cranmer as archbishop. This was finally achieved in March 1533, despite Eustache Chapuys's sterling efforts to block the eleven papal bulls authorising his consecration. The next task was to forbid unauthorised preaching in order to subdue opposition. After this Cranmer wrote to Henry accusing him of creating a public scandal in having married Katherine of Aragon. He offered the King the opportunity to salve his conscience by appearing in front of an ecclesiastical court. Henry took advantage of this opportunity, but Katherine, who had been similarly invited, refused to attend. The Queen being pronounced contumacious, the verdict was given soon afterwards. Henry's marriage to Katherine was declared null and void on 23 May 1533. Five days later, on 28 May, Cranmer declared the marriage between Henry and Anne valid. All that remained now was to arrange the coronation.

Despite the support and the apparent good will that surrounded Henry's marriage to Anne at this time, there were those who remained firmly against it. Anne Boleyn's earliest biographer, George Wyatt, the grandson of the famous poet, relates a sinister story of a book of old prophecies which had mysteriously found its way into Anne's chamber. It featured three figures marked H, K and A, signifying King Henry, Katherine and Anne. Upon discovering the book, Anne called to her maid, saying,

'Come hither, Nan... see here a book of prophecy; this he saith is the king, this the queen, mourning, weeping and wringing her hands, and this is myself with my head off.' The maid answered, 'If I thought it true, though he were an emperor, I would not marry him with that condition.' 'Yes, Nan,' replied the lady, 'I think the book a bauble; yet for the hope I have that the realm may be happy by my issue, I am resolved to have him whatsoever might become of me.'[3]

'Nan' was Anne Gainsford, a former attendant to Anne Boleyn, who recalled this anecdote and others to George Wyatt, who wrote them into his *The Life of Queen Anne Boleigne*.

There were other prophecies too. These were not aimed specifically at Anne but at the Boleyn family as a whole. Mistress Amadas spoke of how she rejoiced when the Tower was painted white for it meant that, shortly afterwards, 'my Lady Anne should be burned, for she is a harlot; that Master Nores [Norris] was bawd between the king and her; that the king had kept both the mother and the daughter, and that my lord of Wiltshire was bawd both to his wife and his two daughters'.[4]

As noted previously, Mistress Amadas might have been Henry's mistress for a time. After she was abandoned by her husband she began to champion the causes of other discarded wives, in this case Queen Katherine. Her pronouncements are significant. In one she states that 'there was never a good married woman in England except Prince Arthur's dowager, the Duchess of Norfolk, and herself' and that the Emperor Charles would deliver all good wives when he came, which she expected would be soon. Prince Arthur's dowager is, of course, Queen Katherine. The Duchess of Norfolk is Elizabeth, the daughter of Edward Stafford, the third Duke of Buckingham. Elizabeth had been put aside by Norfolk whose mistress was Elizabeth, or Bess, Holland.

Mistress Amadas's accusation that Henry had kept both Mary and her mother is supported in a letter written to Henry

VIII by Sir George Throckmorton. Sir George, the staunchly Catholic member of parliament for Warwickshire, opposed the annulment of Henry's marriage to Katherine. Although the letter was written in 1537 it speaks of events some six or seven years previously. Throckmorton had been sent for by the King after speaking about the Act in Restraint of Appeals,

> and seeing that the king's conscience was troubled about having married his brother's wife, said to him, 'I feared if ye did marry Queen Anne your conscience would be more troubled at length, for it is thought ye have meddled both with the mother and the sister.' To this the king replied, 'never with the mother.' At this my lord Privy Seal [Thomas Cromwell] standing nearby said 'Nor never with the sister either, and therefore put that out of your mind.'[5]

The Catholic rhetoric had already begun and it would gain momentum as time went by. Henry would eventually be accused of being Anne Boleyn's father[6] which is clearly impossible if for no other reason than that he was still only a boy at the time of her birth. It is to the disparaging of Henry over his relationship with Anne Boleyn that we must look for the origins of these scandals. Not only was she the sister of his former mistress, she was also seen to have usurped the place of Queen Katherine. In view of this, although Cromwell was wrong to assert that Henry had never had an affair with Mary Boleyn, he can be forgiven if his motive was to protect his King's reputation.

Mistress Amadas's anger at her treatment by her husband must also be taken into account. However, since almost nothing is known of her affair with Henry, if it existed at all, we cannot speculate that her wrath towards the Boleyns stemmed from her having been discarded in favour of Mary.

Vicious though such prophecies were, they had little significance, for the time being at least. Anne was married to Henry and was pregnant with what everyone was convinced would be a son. It remained now to crown her Queen of England.

At about five o'clock in the afternoon of 31 May 1533 Anne Boleyn set out in procession from the Tower to Westminster. She was dressed resplendently after the French fashion. Her surcoat and mantle were of white tissue, the mantle furred with ermine. She mounted a litter covered inside and out with white satin and drawn by two palfreys in white damask. A canopy of cloth of gold was held over her as she made her way through the streets. Behind her were ladies on hackneys, others riding in gilded coaches. Mary, wearing a gown made of seven yards of scarlet velvet, sat in the third coach accompanied by her mother, Lady Elizabeth Boleyn, Countess of Wiltshire. Lady Fitzwarren, Mistress Mary Zouche, Mistress Margery Horsman and Alice Parker, Lady Morley, the mother of George Boleyn's wife, Jane, shared the coach.

The procession was a spectacular sight, a riot of colour and pageantry. In each open space along the way a mystery was performed. Wine flowed from the fountains; the Cross of Cheapside, the Eleanor Cross and the conduits of Fleet Street, Ludgate and Temple Bar were newly repaired and decorated. The Master Baker met Anne, presenting her with 1,000 marks in the name of the city. Schoolchildren stood on a platform at the east end of St Paul's and recited poetry in honour of the King and the new Queen.

Arriving at Westminster Hall, Anne left her litter and went to sit at the high dais beneath the cloth of estate. Here she was served with spice, 'suttilties', hypocras and other wines. She then withdrew to her chamber at York Place to refresh herself in readiness for a rendezvous with Henry at Westminster.

The following day, Sunday 1 June, was Anne Boleyn's coronation day. Mary attended her as she had the day before. Wearing a gown of scarlet, a cloak furred with ermine and a bonnet, she stood behind the new Queen as she was crowned, unusually, with King Edward's Crown and enthroned on King Edward's throne. King Henry was also in attendance but, as was the custom when a Queen was crowned in a separate ceremony, he watched from behind a screen in order not to divert attention away from her.

The ceremony over, it was now time for the banquet.[7] The Great Hall at Westminster was richly decorated with arras. A table, reached by twelve steps, was set for the new Queen at the upper end of the hall. Anne, sitting beneath a rich cloth of estate, dined in full view of everyone. Four tables were arranged along the length of the hall, the first being occupied by duchesses, countesses and ladies. At the second table were the gentlemen of the court. The third table was that of the Mayor of London, who sat with the Aldermen. At the fourth table were the Barons of the Cinque Ports and the masters of the chancellery.

At the entrance to the hall, conduits poured out wine, while fine meats, spices and other delicacies were served on gilt dishes. These were offered first to Anne before being passed down to the guests. Gaiety and laughter accompanied the sweet sounds of the minstrels, the odd cheer and the spectacular sight of the Duke of Suffolk, gorgeously dressed, his costume studded with many precious stones and pearls, riding up and down on a courser caparisoned in crimson velvet. Once again King Henry watched from a hidden place; the day was Anne's and he would not spoil her royal moment of glory.

It did not end there. With Anne now established as Henry's wife and Queen, the next event to look forward to was the birth of their first child. It seems that Anne's pregnancy began well but that the advanced stages were more difficult. It was even said that the King despaired of her life at one stage, even hoping for a miscarriage if it would save her.[8] In the event, however, everything went smoothly. Anne took to her chamber where, on 7 September 1533, she gave birth.

Like many of their contemporaries who awaited the birth of a child, Anne and Henry had consulted doctors, astrologers, sorcerers and sorceresses; they were told that the baby Anne was carrying was a boy. Henry was delighted. At last he would have his much longed-for heir. However, the baby was not a boy, but a girl. She was beautiful and healthy and her parents named her Elizabeth after Henry's mother as well as Anne's.

The birth of a daughter has been interpreted as a disaster for Anne who, it was felt, showed herself unable to fulfil her duty and provide the King with a male heir. Certainly Eustache Chapuys thought so. Referring to Anne as Henry's mistress because he refused to acknowledge the legality of their marriage, he gleefully wrote to Charles V that 'the King's mistress was delivered of a daughter, to the great regret both of him and the lady'.[9]

However, the birth of Elizabeth, while an anti-climax, was not such a disaster. That she was healthy showed that Anne could carry a baby successfully to term; having done so with her first child, she would no doubt do the same with others. Had not her sister, Mary, given birth to a girl before going on to have a son? Both her children were healthy; there was no reason why it should not be the same for Anne. Indeed, it was not long before Anne appeared to be pregnant again and, as the royal couple looked forward to the birth of a boy, Mary would spring a surprise of her own.

CHAPTER 11

Second Marriage, 'love overcame reason', 1534–1536

What earthy thing more can I crave?

What would I wish more at my will?

Nothing on earth more would I have,

Save that I have, to have it still.

The year 1534 was an important one in the affairs of the Boleyns. Bills ratifying the marriage of Henry and Anne were read in March. Also that month the Act of Succession was passed meaning that the crown would be settled on the children of King Henry and Queen Anne. On 23 June, George Boleyn was made Warden of the Cinque Ports. Anne was the brightest star in the firmament; George was basking in her light and reaping the rewards of the King's good will. All eyes were on the Boleyns, although not all of them were friendly. Any scandal would be seized upon by their enemies, blown out of proportion and used against them. Imagine the reaction at court, then, when a radiant Mary suddenly appeared in September, obviously pregnant, and announced that she had taken a new husband.

Mary had remarried in a secret ceremony. Because she had acted without the knowledge or approval of her family, it is reasonable to assume that this was a love match. Although now in her early thirties and no longer young by the standards of her day, Mary had preserved her beauty and had once again caught the eye of a handsome man. Just as she had with King Henry, Mary had lost her heart. This time, however, she was free to take the relationship to its fullest flowering. Just like her former mistress, the French Queen, all those years ago, she had thrown all caution to the winds and followed where her heart led her. In marrying so precipitously Mary clearly forgot the lessons she had learned at her mother's knee:

> If any man bids thee worship and would bed thee
> Look that thou scorn him not, what-so-ever he be
> But show it to thy friends, and conceal thou it nought
> Sit not by him, neither stand, there sin might be wrought[1]

The object of Mary's love was William Stafford, a soldier in the garrison at Calais and one of King Henry's gentlemen ushers. He was also a distant relative of the fallen Edward Stafford, third Duke of Buckingham. His name crops up from time to time in the archives, such as in 1526 when he is named as a freeholder of the Manor of Tickford.[2] A year later he and others were commissioned to search barns and stacks in the county of Berkshire. The object of the search is now lost, but it was probably linked to the order that they were to execute the statute of Winchester against vagabonds and unlawful games. In April 1529 Stafford and Richard

Andrewes purchased the marriage and lands of the King's ward, William Somer, for 20 marks.[3] In November of that year Stafford was appointed Sheriff of Oxfordshire and Berkshire in company with John Brome and Henry Bruges.[4]

When Mary met William Stafford is impossible to say. It might have been at the time of her visit to Calais with Henry and Anne in the autumn of 1532. If not, she perhaps caught his attention at Anne's coronation the following year, where Stafford's name is found among those appointed as 'sewers'.[5] On the other hand, his presence at court since at least 1526 might indicate that they had known each other for some time.

Whatever the case, it is clear that Mary had maintained some link to the garrison at Calais following her visit. In February 1534 she wrote a letter to Lord Lisle:

> I desire you and my good lady to be good unto Thomas Hunt, a poor man at Calais, for the room of soldier [*sic*] with 6d a day in the King's retinue, when any such is vacant. From the King's manor of York Place at Westminster, 13 Feb.[6]

The letter is signed by Mary Carey and is countersigned by Sir William Kingston. The position of Mary's signature, to the right and slightly above that of Sir William, suggests that she is the original writer. This is one of only two of Mary's letters to have survived and, short though it is, it imparts a wealth of information.

The recipient is Arthur Plantagenet, Viscount Lisle, Governor of Calais. The beneficiary of Mary's request is Thomas Hunt, a soldier from Calais for whom Mary is trying to find employment and lodgings, thus continuing the connection with the garrison there. Nothing more is known about Thomas Hunt, although it is possible that he is the same man who became the guardian of the soldier and conspirator Sir Peter Carew. As a soldier he might have known William Stafford. Perhaps Mary was even writing at Stafford's request.

The countersignature is that of Sir William Kingston. This man would play such an important part in the last days of Mary's sister, Anne. At the date this letter was written Kingston was a knight of the shire for Gloucestershire, Constable of the Tower of London and a councillor. He was a friend of Lord Lisle. Moreover, although his early background is hazy, it is believed that Kingston had some family connection with Edward Stafford, third Duke of Buckingham. As such, he was related in some way to William Stafford.

The letter was written at Henry's manor of York Place. This, as we know, was one of Anne Boleyn's favourite residences. This, therefore, supports the theory that Mary and Anne had remained close and that Mary formed part of Anne's royal entourage.

William Stafford is associated with Lady Lisle, in whose service he appears to have been. A letter to Lady Lisle mentions Stafford, placing him in London in August 1534 and describing him as her servant. This, in turn, is consistent with his Calais connection.

Calais was significant to Mary in another respect as well. It had strong connections to her religious sympathies. It is well known that the Boleyn family were staunch defenders of the reform movement. Chapuys once famously stated that the Boleyns were 'more Lutheran that Luther'.[7] While this is probably something of an exaggeration, he is correct in asserting their support for the King's break with Rome which, in his eyes, probably equated with Lutheranism.

Arguably the most committed members of the Boleyn family to the evangelical cause were Anne and George. George's advocacy of religious reform was well known. He worked in tandem with other royal officials in support of Henry's claim to be supreme head of the Church in England and it was he who promoted the King's position in convocation. He was also acknowledged as one of Henry's principal advisors in the cause of religious reform. Fully supportive of the submission of the clergy, he worked diligently with the upper house of convocation to manage the final phases of the process.

George's zeal for reform might be seen as being linked to Anne's cause and the gains to be made from her elevation. Nevertheless, it can be accepted that his faith was genuine and strong and that his efforts were driven by deeply personal conviction. He commissioned two texts, both authored by French reformers, which advocated making scripture accessible to laymen without the necessity for translation and interpretation by priests. These were presented to Anne, who also owned and read bibles in French and in English. Such works had to be smuggled into England because they were considered heretical and ownership of them was illegal. As such, George took full advantage of his diplomatic visits to France and the contacts he made there and at Calais to enable him to carry out his mission.

This, then, brought him into the sphere of William Stafford, soon to be his brother-in-law. While the connection seems tenuous and the only direct link between George Boleyn and William Stafford is Mary, it is known that Stafford was as zealous for religious reform as his Boleyn in-laws. In later years, after Mary's death, he would be imprisoned in the Fleet for eating meat on Good Friday. He and his second wife, Dorothy, would be among the Marian exiles, joining the English church in Geneva and living in close proximity to John Calvin. Their son, John, born at Geneva on 4 January 1556, was probably named after Calvin, who stood as godfather to the child. William Stafford would never see England again; he would die a few months after his arrival at Geneva.

It is tempting to think that this is all of a piece with Mary's own religious outlook. She belonged to a family whose reformist sympathies played such a major role in their lives. Such sentiment was continued into the next generation, as her son, having been made the ward of Anne, was certain to be educated as an evangelical. Sadly, Mary's own feelings on the subject, overshadowed as they were by those of her more celebrated siblings, can never be known.

While the Boleyns would have had no objection to William Stafford's religious outlook, they certainly did not approve of his social position. Stafford came from a good Midlands family. Nevertheless, the branch to which he belonged was impoverished and considered far beneath their more illustrious relatives in terms of status. He was considerably lower than Mary in rank and expectations. This, and the fact that Mary had married him without permission, would have been enough to incur her family's disfavour. In making such a *mésalliance*, Mary had acted in a manner unbecoming to her position as the Queen's sister. That her family had made no attempt to find her a new husband notwithstanding, she should have expected to be married to a person of high station, a man whose position and family connections would have been of advantage to the Boleyn family. What was even more serious, however, is that Mary had undermined Anne's position by not taking into account the presiding role that the Boleyn family now owed to Anne as Queen.

It has been suggested that Sir Thomas Boleyn had disapproved of Mary's marriage to William Stafford on the additional grounds that she had become pregnant before the marriage.[8] This might have been so but, since it is not known when Mary and Stafford were married, such an assertion should be treated with caution. Moreover, Mary appears to have had no difficulty in getting pregnant when she wanted to and it is equally possible that the child she now carried was conceived soon after her marriage.

However, Mary's pregnancy and, perhaps more importantly, the point in time at which it occurred, was of major significance. The timing of Mary's appearance at court, newly married and clearly pregnant, could not have been worse. Something had gone wrong with Anne's pregnancy. The exact details cannot be discerned because the secrecy that surrounded it is virtually impenetrable to this day. Chapuys mentioned the pregnancy in his dispatch to Charles V on 28 January 1534.[9] Six months later he noted that Anne was unable to travel to France on account of her condition.[10] Certainly, she must have been quite advanced by July, when the strain of a sea-crossing must have posed a risk to her and the baby.

Since nothing came of this pregnancy it is generally believed that Anne had miscarried and that she and Henry, away on their summer progress, had decided to keep the matter quiet. Since they were attended by a minimum of staff, this was perfectly possible. Even Chapuys, who had been separated from the court during this time, could not be certain about what had occurred. It could be that Anne had simply been mistaken. On the other hand, it has been speculated that it was not a pregnancy at all, but a pseudocyesis, a phantom pregnancy caused by Anne's desperation to give Henry his heir.[11]

Anne's anxiety was fully justified for, as Chapuys goes on to say, Henry had no scruples about taking up once again with a mysterious lady with whom he seems to have fallen in love. The ambassador goes further. His dispatch makes it clear that Anne had attempted to send the lady away, for which she had incurred Henry's wrath. Chapuys was confident that not too much importance should be attached to this quarrel because 'of the craft of the said lady [Anne], who knows well how to manage him [Henry]'.[12]

Nevertheless, cracks were beginning to appear in the royal marriage and the danger to Anne was all too obvious. Mary's pregnancy served only to heighten her sister's predicament. Therefore, for this, as well as for her recklessness in forming such an unsuitable marriage, Mary was banished from court. The attentive Chapuys summed up the situation in a dispatch to his master on 19 December 1534:

> The Lady's sister [Mary] was also banished from Court three months ago, but it was necessary to do so, for besides that she had been found guilty of misconduct, it would not have been becoming to see her at Court *enceint*.[13]

So Mary was sent to the country away from the court, far from the influence of the King and the Queen, away from the glittering life of poetry, music, dancing and laughter. Moreover, Sir Thomas Boleyn had cut off Mary's allowance, leaving her without a penny. This was only to be expected; Sir Thomas Boleyn's parsimony was legendary. In 1530, when he was enjoying the revenues and advantages that came with being the Earl of Wiltshire, he wrote to a servant of Lord Lisle to ask for the return of a basin and ewer he had lent him or else to send the price, which was £18 10s because, as he claimed, he was 'a poor man'.[14]

Now, just as he had neglected his eldest daughter following the death of her first husband, he refused to help her because she had taken a second without consulting her family. So desperate was Mary's situation that she wrote to the only person she though would help her. The second of the two letters remaining from Mary, then, was to Thomas Cromwell. In it she begs him to intercede with the King on her behalf and that of her husband:

Master secretary,

After my poor recommendations, which is smally to be regarded of me, that I am a poor banished creature, this shall be to desire you to be good to my poor husband and to me. I am sure it is not unknown to you the high displeasure that both he and I have, both of the king's highness and the queen's grace, by reason of our marriage without their knowledge, wherein we both do yield ourselves faulty, and do acknowledge that we did not well to be so hasty nor so bold, without their knowledge. But one thing, good master secretary, consider, that he was young, and love overcame reason; and for my part I saw so much honesty in him, that I loved him as well as he did me, and was in bondage, and glad I was to be at liberty: so that, for my part, I saw that all the world did set so little by me, and he so much, that I thought I could take no better way but to take him and to forsake all other ways, and live a poor, honest life with him. And so I do put no doubts but we should, if we might once be so happy to recover the king's gracious favour and the queen's. For well I might have had a greater man of birth and a higher, but I assure you I could never have had one that should have loved me so well, nor a more honest man; and besides that, he is both come of an ancient stock, and again as meet (if it was his grace's pleasure) to do the king service, as any young gentleman in his court.

Therefore, good master secretary, this shall be my suit to you, that, for the love that I well know you do bear to all my blood, though, for my part, I have not deserved it but smally, by reason of my vile conditions, as to put my husband to the king's grace that he may do his duty as all other gentlemen do. And, good master secretary, sue us to the king's highness, and beseech his highness, which ever was wont to take pity, to have pity on us; and that it will please his grace of his goodness to speak to the queen's grace for us; for, so far as I can perceive, her grace is so highly displeased with us both that, without the king be so good lord to us as to withdraw his rigour and sue for us, we are never like to recover her grace's favour: which is too heavy to bear. And seeing there is no remedy, for God's sake help us; for we have now been a quarter of a year married, I thank God, and too late now to call that again; wherefore it is the more *almones* (alms) to help. But if I were at my liberty and might choose, I ensure you, master secretary, for my little time, I have tried so much honesty to be in him, that I had rather beg my bread with him than to be the greatest queen in Christendom. And I believe verily he is in the same case with me; for I believe verily he would not forsake me to be a king.

Therefore, good master secretary, seeing we are so well together and does [*sic*] intend to live so honest a life, though it be but poor, show part of your goodness to us as well as you do to all the world besides; for I promise you, you have the name to help all them that hath need, and amongst all your suitors I dare be bold to say that you have no matter more to be pitied than ours; and therefore, for God's sake, be good to us, for in you is all our trust.

And I beseech you, good master secretary, pray my lord my father and my lady to be so good to us, and to let me have their blessings and my husband their good will; and I will never desire more of them. Also, I pray you, desire my lord of Norfolk and my lord my brother to be good to us. I dare not write to them, they are so cruel against us; but if, with any pain that I could take with my life, I might win their good wills, I promise you there is no child living would venture more than I. And so I pray you to report by me, and you shall find my writing true, and in all points which I may please them in I shall be ready to obey them nearest my husband, whom I am most bound to; to whom I most heartily beseech you to be good unto, which, for my sake, is a poor banished man for an honest and a godly cause. And seeing that I have read in old books that some, for as just causes, have by kings and queens been pardoned by the suit of good folks, I trust it shall be our chance, through your good help, to come to the same; as knoweth the (Lord) God, who send you health and heart's ease. Scribbled by her ill hand, who is your poor, humble suitor, always to command, Mary Stafford.[15]

Mary explains to Cromwell that her problems stemmed from her having married William Stafford without the consent of her family and she freely admits her wrongdoing. She speaks of how she had been kept under tight control, or bondage, by her family and that her marriage was her way to freedom. This did not mean that she entered into marriage simply to escape her family. She notes that Stafford was so young and that 'love overcame reason' that neither of them could help themselves. She indicates more than once that they were deeply in love and that their love was mutual; should she be given her time again, she adds, she would have made the same decision to marry Stafford.

Clearly Mary felt that her family had kept her on too tight a rein, but how much of this was true and how much her own imagination? Following the death of her first husband, William Carey, Mary had been taken in by her father, albeit with great reluctance on his part. Since that time she had remained at court at least periodically, even accompanying her sister to Calais. Yet, she still managed to appear at court, obviously pregnant and announcing that she had married. Now, in her letter to Cromwell, she writes that she had been married 'a quarter of a year'. That she had been at liberty to be courted by a man, to fall in love with him, to marry him in secrecy and then to become pregnant by him would suggest that her family had, in fact, neglected Mary rather than kept a tight rein on her. Their primary concern was Anne, and Mary was left out. They had not even attempted to find her a new husband. As such, Mary took matters into her own hands and married a man with whom she had fallen in love.

Mary goes on to highlight William Stafford's good family connections, noting that he is of 'ancient stock'. This is a reference to his being related to the Stafford Dukes of Buckingham. As such, as Mary asserts, William's rightful place is at court.

Mary then appeals to Cromwell's love for her family. This was underpinned by their shared interest in religious reform. Cromwell, like the Boleyns, was an evangelical, albeit a recent convert. He had supported the idea, promoted by Anne Boleyn and her circle, of the assertion of royal supremacy over the church. This had, of course, helped smooth the way for the dissolution of Henry's marriage to Katherine of Aragon and his subsequent marriage to Anne.

Mary notes that Henry had always been 'wont to take pity' on her. She almost certainly refers to the assistance previously given to her by the King following the death of William Carey. Mary, facing severe financial difficulties, had appealed to Anne, who had then presented her sister's case to Henry. The outcome was, as we have seen, that Henry intervened on Mary's behalf and ordered her father to take her under his roof and support her.

However, this time, Mary's real concern was the fact that she had become estranged from Anne. In a way, this should not have been unexpected. Mary's disregard for Anne's position notwithstanding, she had shown herself capable of successful pregnancies and had already given birth to a healthy son. Anne, on the other hand, had managed to produce a daughter and had just suffered a failed pregnancy. Still, Anne had been instrumental in helping Mary last time; this time she would not. Now Mary was sent to face the future away from her family, the court and the King with only the love of her young husband to sustain her. As such, her statement 'I had rather beg my bread with him than to be the greatest queen in Christendom' could have been born of a fit of pique. On the other hand, and more seriously, Mary is possibly commenting on the legality, or the morality, of Anne's marriage to Henry, in comparison with which her marriage to William Stafford is at least honest.

Cromwell's reply to Mary, if there was one, has not survived and the outcome of her plea is not known. Nevertheless, Cromwell had a reputation for assisting women in Mary's situation. It is probably safe to suggest that her plight had been brought to the notice of Henry, who again took up her cause as he had in the first days of her widowhood.

What became of Mary's baby is equally unknown. No trace of it exists, making it probable that the pregnancy ended in miscarriage or that the child died young. A child sometimes mentioned as having been born to Mary and William, a boy named Edward is, in fact, Stafford's son by his second wife, Dorothy.

It is often thought that Mary's banishment lasted until after the downfall of her family and the executions of her sister and brother. Future events will show that this was not the case. The Staffords' rural exile was not to last so very long; perhaps due to Thomas Cromwell's efforts. Mary would continue to be a feature in the life of her sister, although Anne's brilliance inevitably ensured that Mary would always remain in the shadows.

CHAPTER 12

These Bloody Days, 1536

These bloody days have broken my heart.

My lust, my youth did them depart,

And blind desire of estate.

Who hastes to climb seeks to revert.

Of truth, *circa Regna tonat*.

Life and death merged at the dawning of the year 1536. Katherine of Aragon clung doggedly to her former status as Henry's wife and Queen, and she insisted that everyone should treat her as such. Still, the past nine years had taken their toll physically and emotionally. Now, in the cold greyness of early January, she knew that she was approaching the end of her torment.

In fact, Katherine had been ill for some time. Ambassador Chapuys, her loyal friend and champion, obtained permission to visit her in exile at Kimbolton, but as he was preparing to set out Henry advised him that Katherine was dying and that, if the ambassador were to make the journey, he probably would not arrive in time to see her. Chapuys ignored Henry's advice and took to horse, arriving at Kimbolton on 2 January.

As he approached the bed where Katherine lay, the ambassador's heart went out to her. Katherine was too weak even to sit up to receive him. Yet, as he began to speak to her, Katherine seemed to derive strength from him; his very presence acted as a tonic to her. Chapuys stayed at Kimbolton for four days, although his greatest fear was that his interviews, lasting some two hours each day, would drain her. Also, he was cautious of abusing the licence Henry had given him to visit Katherine. Chapuys left Kimbolton on 5 January taking a leisurely pace in case he should be recalled. The following day Katherine went into a rapid decline. She died on 7 January.

Life went on. At court, the Boleyns were celebrating Anne's new pregnancy. She and Henry had gone on their summer progress to the Severn the previous summer. As they slowly made their way back towards Windsor, they stopped in Hampshire, where they remained for most of September and October. It was a happy and carefree time. They had hunted and danced, they had dropped in on the Seymours. In this honeymoon atmosphere, Anne had conceived again; this time, it would be a boy.

As the debris of the Christmas and New Year festivities were still being cleared away, news came of Katherine's death. Henry and Anne reacted each in their own way. For the myth that Henry wept over a last letter written to him by Katherine from her death bed and that it was Anne and not Henry who dressed in yellow we must look to the later recusant tradition. Chapuys's dispatches and Henry's own behaviour make it perfectly clear how the King received the news of the death of the woman who had been the centre of his world for the best part of twenty years.

For Henry, quite simply, it was the best news he could have received. 'God be praised', he exclaimed, 'that we are free from all suspicion of war.'¹ His jubilation was shared by the Boleyns. Sir Thomas and Lord Rochford thought it a pity that Princess Mary had not accompanied her mother.

The next day was Sunday and mass at the Chapel Royal was infused with a buoyant spirit. Henry dressed from head to toe in yellow except for a jaunty white feather in his bonnet. Elizabeth, who had been staying with her parents for the festive season, was shown off to fawning courtiers. Then Henry celebrated in the only way he knew how: he hurriedly organised a joust. He had been given a new lease of life. He was a young man again.

Anne's thoughts were more mixed. At first she was ecstatic, even generously rewarding the messenger who had broken the news of Katherine's death to her. Later, according to Chapuys, the reality of it all hit home. She frequently wept and feared that the King might do to her as he had done to Katherine.² The ambassador also heard that Henry had confided to someone that his marriage to Anne was the result of his having been seduced by witchcraft and, for that reason, he considered it null. The evidence was that God did not permit them to have a male child. Henry then expressed his intention to take another wife.

Chapuys treated this news with caution even though it came from an impeccable source. He was right to do so. Anne was pregnant and, as usual, Henry's optimism allowed him to believe that she would give him his Prince of Wales. In fact, his high spirits had not yet calmed when, on 24 January, he went jousting.

What happened next is disputed. The Bishop of Faenza reported that Henry fell from his horse 'and was thought to be dead for two hours'.[3] Chapuys wrote that the King was mounted on a great horse to run at the lists when 'both fell so heavily that everyone thought it a miracle that he was not killed, but he sustained no injury'. Anne had not witnessed the incident and her uncle, the Duke of Norfolk, broke the news to her. Emotions ran high.

It cannot be said that Mary was on hand to comfort her sister but, five days later, when disaster struck, she most certainly was at Anne's side. On 29 January, the very day that Katherine of Aragon was laid to rest, Anne miscarried. The three and a half month old foetus 'seemed to be a male child, at which the King has shown great distress.'[4]

It was said that Anne consoled her maids, who wept at the loss of the child. She told them that the miscarriage had been for the best because she would be the sooner with child again. The son she would bear would not be doubtful like this one, which had been conceived while Katherine was still alive.

Chapuys interpreted this as acknowledgement on Anne's part of doubts about the legitimacy of her daughter.[5] It coincided with a rumour which held that the Queen was unable to conceive and that 'the daughter said to be hers and the abortion the other day are supposititious'.[6] In other words, the Princess Elizabeth was not the daughter of Anne who was, in fact, unable to conceive.

This gossip was also known to the Bishop of Faenza, who notes 'that woman' pretended to have miscarried of a son, not being really with child, and, to keep up the deceit, would allow no one to attend on her but her sister.[7]

Here we have the only piece of evidence that places Mary at court with Queen Anne at a time she was commonly believed to have been banished to the country. It is also from the bishop's dispatch that we learn of King François's assessment of Mary as a great prostitute, worse than the others. The implication here is that because Mary was of dubious reputation in the eyes of the French King, so Anne must also be tainted with sin. Also, while Mary had such a reputation for licentiousness yet did not produce a brood of illegitimate children, it is probable that she was aware of some form of birth control. In this respect that which can serve to avoid pregnancy can be reversed to encourage it. It is possible that Mary was passing on her knowledge in such matters to her sister. Childbirth was, after all, the exclusive realm of women, who would be free to carry out any illicit and devious activities beyond the control of men.

However, the bishop's assessment of the situation is insupportable. If Anne really did feel as vulnerable as these dispatches suggest, it would have been foolish beyond belief that she should invent a pregnancy only to be found out in the end. We can attribute such talk to Anne's enemies. Equally, we can be sure that Elizabeth was indeed Anne's own daughter and that the pregnancy that ended in miscarriage in January 1536 was genuine.

Anne's miscarriage was attributed to shock over the news of Henry's accident as well as 'that the love she bore him was far greater than that of the late Queen. So that her heart broke when she saw that he [Henry] loved others.'[8] Anne spoke of 'others' in the plural, but only one of them would prove to be a danger to her. In Chapuys's dispatch of 10 February, he mentions a lady at the court named Mistress Semel, by which he means Jane Seymour. This is the first appearance in Chapuys's dispatches of the woman who was to become Henry's third wife.

When Anne's fall from grace came, it did so with remarkable speed. For a long while after the miscarriage she remained strong at court. Thomas Cromwell continued as her supporter. Although a faction had formed to try to persuade Henry to divorce Anne and replace her with Jane Seymour, it was clear at this stage that Henry had no intention of doing so. He remained committed to Anne; his desire with respect to Jane was to make her his mistress. As to Anne, Henry worked tirelessly to have his marriage acknowledged abroad and to see Anne recognised as Queen.

The trouble, when it did come, originated not in Anne's relationship with Henry but in her relationship with Thomas Cromwell. It was initiated by a dispute over the assets of the dissolved monasteries. Anne wanted them to go to educational and charitable causes. Cromwell saw a better use for them in the royal treasury.

On Passion Sunday, 2 April 1536, Anne's almoner, John Skip, preached a passionate sermon in which Thomas

Cromwell was likened to Haman, the tyrannical councillor of King Ahasuerus in the *Book of Esther*. Haman, it will be remembered, was behind the organisation of a pogrom and who, when his plan was thwarted by Esther, was hanged. Skip's sermon contained parallels to the major players in the dissolution of the monasteries. Henry was King Ahasuerus; Anne was Esther, Cromwell was Haman and the Jews, whom Haman had wanted to destroy, were the clergy, especially the monastic clergy, who were about to be despoiled. The threat to Cromwell was all too clear.

More than this, however, was Henry's attitude towards the proposal to abandon England's reliance on French goodwill and to enter into a *rapprochement* with the Emperor Charles V instead. This had been put forward by Chapuys and was fully endorsed by Cromwell. Although the proposal specified legitimising Princess Mary, it still had the backing of the Boleyns because she would come after those children born to Henry and Anne. For once the Boleyns were in step with the conservative faction at court and there was unity of support for the *rapprochement*.

A meeting was arranged between Henry and Charles's ambassador, Chapuys. However, things did not work out as Cromwell had anticipated. Henry had no intention of entering into negotiations. He used the meeting to press for Charles's recognition of his marriage and his acceptance of Anne as his Queen. Henry even manoeuvred Chapuys into the awkward position of acknowledging Anne, which was something the ambassador had always avoided doing. Cromwell was so upset by Henry's stance that he took to his bed. Following the threat to him, veiled beneath the Haman reference, and with his political position seriously undermined, he came to the realisation that Anne would have to be removed.

Cromwell now turned his back on the Boleyns, favouring the Seymours and their conservative backers instead. Next he set about destroying Henry's love for, and trust in, Anne. He also took advantage of the situation by seeking to remove his principal rival at court, Henry Norris. A loyal and trusted servant, Norris was probably the closest thing Henry had to a true friend. To Cromwell he was an obstacle to be got rid of. The evidence was not far to seek, nor was it necessary to invent it; a bit of manipulation of events would be all that was needed.

Cromwell took full advantage of a very public altercation that took place in Anne's apartments. For a while Norris had been courting a lady by the name of Margaret, or Madge, Shelton, a cousin to Mary and Anne. For some reason he had not taken the plunge. Anne asked him why not. He answered that he preferred to wait a while. At this point Anne, somewhat irritated, accused Norris of looking for dead men's shoes for, if anything but good came to the King, Norris would look to have Anne. Shocked, Norris replied that if he should have any such thought he would prefer his head to be cut off.[9] While this was certainly incriminating to Anne, it was not to Norris, but it was to seal his fate anyway.

Still, Norris was not the only quarry in Cromwell's hunt. Anne's court was one of liveliness and flirtation, where courtly love reigned supreme against a background of laughter and frivolity. Cromwell soon found what he was looking for. A court musician, Mark Smeaton, was arrested. Under torture, or the threat of it, he confessed to adultery with the Queen. Armed with his 'evidence' Cromwell alerted Henry to the situation on May Day, the very day of the year when courtly love was most lavishly celebrated. Henry immediately broke off the joust. He offered Norris, who had been riding in the lists, pardon if he would confess to adultery with Anne. Innocent, Norris refused and was sent to the Tower.

Events now moved quickly. The following day Anne was arrested. Since her brother, George, was capable and intelligent, and would be expected to mount an energetic defence of his sister, he was arrested too. Within the week four courtiers, alleged lovers of the Queen, were committed to the Tower: Francis Weston, William Brereton, Thomas Wyatt and Richard Page. Archbishop Cranmer and others were kept out of Henry's way until it was too late for them to intervene on Anne's behalf.

Against established tradition and right, the trials, when they began, opened with those of the commoners. The jury, hand-picked by Cromwell, had little difficulty in finding Norris, Weston, Brereton and Smeaton guilty of high treason, even though adultery with a Queen would not formally attract such a charge for another six years. If they were guilty then, by definition, so was Anne. In George's case, the charge of adultery was augmented by the still more abhorrent charge of incest, evidence for which was said to have been provided by his wife, Jane. It was a foregone conclusion. All those who had been arrested, except for Thomas Wyatt and Richard Page, who did not even undergo trial, were condemned to death. George Boleyn was beheaded on 17 May 1536. Norris, Weston, Brereton and Smeaton followed him to the block.

Mary's whereabouts as the tragic events of May 1536 unfolded are not known; it is generally thought that she was living in the country with William Stafford at the time. This is largely due to the belief that she did not return to court after her second marriage. This, as has been shown, was not true. Mary maintained a presence at court; she was with Anne at the time of her miscarriage the previous January. Nevertheless, there is no evidence that she attempted to make contact with Anne or George during their imprisonment and, it must be said, she probably would have been unsuccessful had she done so.

Mary's absence can be accounted for in a number of ways. It could be that she had been sent away by Henry, perhaps for her own protection. The swiftness of the events and the fact that Henry appears to have been kept unaware of any investigation into his wife's activities until the May Day arrests would, however, preclude this. Alternatively, Mary might have been taken away from court by her father, who realised that she would now be his only surviving child.

The necessity that he should be unaware of the imminent arrests, as well as his subsequent behaviour, again, would undermine this theory. There is little to allow us to think that Sir Thomas even considered Mary's welfare in the aftermath of her sister's downfall, at least at first. The most probable explanation is that Mary had gone to her estates in the country, probably on ordinary domestic business, and so was sheltered from the storm that engulfed her family by her distance from it.

Anne Boleyn appears to have assumed that she was to be executed on 17 May 1536. In the end the only executions that took place on that day were those of her brother and her alleged accomplices. The date of her execution had not, in fact, been set because the headsman, from Calais or St Omer, had not arrived. Also time had to be allowed for one final act of cruelty towards Anne: the annulment of her marriage to Henry VIII.[10]

As reported by Ambassador Chapuys,

the Archbishop of Canterbury declared by sentence that the Concubine's daughter was the bastard of Mr Norris, and not the King's daughter... Others tell me that the said Archbishop had pronounced the marriage of the King and Concubine invalid on account of the King having had connection with her sister.[11]

The reason behind Henry's decision to divorce Anne even though she was, by this time, a condemned traitor, was to ensure that he would have an undisputed heir. His marriage to Katherine of Aragon had failed to provide him with one. The Princess Mary had been declared illegitimate on the grounds that her mother had not been Henry's legal wife.

Likewise, Henry's marriage to Anne Boleyn, so filled with hope at the outset, had also proved to be a disappointment, with only a daughter to show for it. Once again, in Henry's view, it became necessary for him to marry again; but it was crucial that the legitimacy of any sons born to him by his next wife could not be disputed. It was necessary to do the thing properly this time.

Firstly, it was essential that the annulment of his marriage to Katherine should not be shown to have been false because that would have restored Princess Mary's legitimacy and reinstated her as heir. There was, however, a way out. The Ecclesiastical Licences Act of 1534 confirmed all dispensations thus far issued as valid, but that future ones were to be issued in England and not Rome. Yet there was a qualification. No dispensation could be issued for causes 'contrary or repugnant to the Holy Scriptures and laws of God'.[12]

It had long been Henry's argument that the dispensation that had allowed him to marry Katherine of Aragon was indeed against Holy Scripture. He had ultimately succeeded in annulling his marriage to Katherine on the grounds that he had been related to her in the first degree of affinity due to her earlier marriage with his brother. The dispensation of 1528 permitted Henry to marry Anne Boleyn in spite of the fact that their union was forbidden due to the same impediment. That is, he had been granted a dispensation to allow him to marry Anne despite his having had a sexual relationship with her sister, Mary. That relationship placed Henry and Anne within the first degree of affinity. Henry had at last come to accept that his marriage to Anne Boleyn, as with his marriage to Katherine of Aragon, was forbidden by divine law as given in Holy Writ for which there could be no dispensation. Anne was not and had never been Henry's legal wife. As a consequence, Princess Elizabeth, like her step-sister, Princess Mary, was illegitimate.

Archbishop Cranmer applied the clause in the Ecclesiastical Licences Act to the dispensation regarding the King's relationship to Mary Boleyn, thus making Henry's marriage to Anne incestuous and invalid. The way was now clear for any children born to him by Jane Seymour, or any subsequent wife, to be accepted as legitimate and to inherit the crown after him. Henry's relationship with Mary Boleyn had been the reason why he and Anne were forbidden to marry; it had now become the means of his final destruction of Anne.

In fact, Henry had already begun proceedings to annul his marriage to Anne Boleyn. As early as 13 May, two days before her trial, Anne's former suitor, Henry Percy, Earl of Northumberland, wrote to Cromwell stating that word had reached him that the supposed pre-contract between himself and Anne was to be resurrected and used against her. Percy denied that such a pre-contract had ever existed, a claim he would maintain 'to my damnation'.[13]

If, in the event, Henry had no legitimate children after all, he still had three illegitimate daughters, the ex-princesses Mary and Elizabeth, and Katherine Carey. He also had two illegitimate sons, Henry Fitzroy and Henry Carey. Should it become necessary to decide which of them should inherit the crown, his sons would naturally take precedence. In fact, Henry Fitzroy was the only one who could be declared as heir. Once again, the relationship with Mary Boleyn, Henry Carey's mother, became an obstacle. It had been an impediment to his marriage to Anne, now that marriage became an impediment to his acknowledging young Carey as his son. As a consequence, Henry Carey would never be accepted as the heir to the throne; he would never be Henry IX.

As to Henry Fitzroy, steps had already been taken to legitimise him. As it happened, the King's efforts were in vain: Henry Fitzroy suddenly became ill and he died of a pulmonary infection only four days after the Succession to the Crown Act of July 1536 was made law.

King Henry's relationship with Mary was also a major factor in the bastardisation of Elizabeth. As has become obvious, the object was not so much to divorce Anne but to bastardise Elizabeth in order to avoid a similar situation to that of Princess Mary. There had to be no doubts regarding the legitimacy of any child Henry had with Jane Seymour. His path finally made smooth, Henry VIII went to dine with Jane and her family on 19 May, the very day his second wife was sent to her death. He and Jane were betrothed the following day.

CHAPTER 13

The Bitter End, 1536–1543

Like as the swan towards her death

Doth strain her voice with doleful note;

Right so sing I with waste of breath,

I die! I die! and you regard it not.

Following the fall of his family, Sir Thomas Boleyn lost his favour with the King. On 29 June his office of Lord Privy Seal went to the architect of his family's ruin, Thomas Cromwell. He was also removed from the commission of the peace for Norfolk, being retained in that office only in the county of Kent.

Still, Sir Thomas did make heroic attempts to regain his position in the royal favour. He continued to give annuities from his estates to the crown. These were used to finance the new generation of court favourites. He assisted in the suppression and punishment of those involved in the Pilgrimage of Grace, the rebellion against the dissolution of the monasteries which broke out during the summer of 1536. He continued to liaise with ministers, while assiduously observing his obligations as a Knight of the Garter.

If all this makes it appear that he had managed to put the past behind him and that his life had returned to normal, this was far from the case. Sir Thomas was deeply distressed and still in shock following the events of the previous weeks. He was grieving for Anne, his beloved daughter, and for George, his only son. What was worse, if anything could be worse, was that Anne's daughter, Elizabeth, had been declared illegitimate; George, although married, had left no children. Sir Thomas had to come to terms with the fact that his name would now die with him.

As the initial shock began to wear off, Sir Thomas gradually came to see a glimmer of light in the darkness into which his world had been plunged. That light was Mary. She was his last surviving child and her children represented the future. He set about a reconciliation, the first step of which was to allow her and William Stafford to use Rochford Hall in Essex. This was to be their principal residence for the remainder of Mary's life.

Sir Thomas was invited to attend the baptism of Prince Edward, Henry's first surviving legitimate son. The prince was born on 15 October 1537 to the woman Anne's death had made way for, Jane Seymour. Such favour inevitably brought with it the hope of restoration, but it was not to be. Piers Butler, whose struggle over the earldom of Ormond seemed lost when the title was granted to Sir Thomas Boleyn, had recently endeared himself to the King for his part in the Kildare rebellion. Sir Thomas's Irish holdings were confiscated and his title of Earl of Ormond was withdrawn by Act of Parliament in 1536. Two years later it was granted to Piers Butler. Upon his death in 1539 it passed to his son,

James, the first of Anne Boleyn's suitors and the man she might have married all those years ago.

Sir Thomas was to retain his Ormond lands in Essex, however, which included Rochford Hall. From these he supported his mother, who received 400 marks from the revenues annually until her death in 1539. Sir Thomas then promised King Henry that he would settle the lands on Elizabeth. In the end, however, he passed them on to Mary and William Stafford.[1]

Mary's mother, Elizabeth Howard, Countess of Wiltshire, withdrew from the court following the disaster that had struck her family. She died in April 1538 at the London residence of Hugh Farringdon, Abbot of Reading Abbey, which stood on the bank of the Thames 'beside Baynard's castle'.[2] A barge draped in black and bearing a white cross, torches ablaze and four banners set at each quarter, carried her across the river to her final resting place at Lambeth.[3]

Following the death of his wife, it was rumoured that Sir Thomas Boleyn would marry Margaret Douglas, King Henry's niece,[4] although nothing came of it. In the end, he was left with nothing but his earldom of Wiltshire to show for a lifetime of loyal service to the King. He retired to Hever and died peacefully in his bed on 12 March 1539. He was buried at St Peter's Church in Hever, his tomb bearing an impressive brass effigy of him wearing the robes of a Knight of the Garter.

George Boleyn's scaffold speech expressed his concerns for religious reform. Such concerns were widespread. It had been feared that, with the fall of Queen Anne, the course of the evangelicals would falter. It was believed by many that Princess Mary would regain her former status and that the King would succumb to the persuasions of the traditionalist faction and return to Rome. Amid this fear, Nicolas Bourbon and other evangelicals returned to France.

While Anne Boleyn's star was rising, her cousin, Sir Francis Bryan, was happy to associate himself with the reform movement, although secretly his sympathies remained conservative. However, following her downfall, when the reform movement appeared weakened, Bryan felt free to follow his conscience. Now Chief Gentleman of the Privy Chamber, he removed Henry Carey and the other royal wards to Woburn Abbey, where he had recently appointed James Prestwich as schoolmaster. Prestwich, who had replaced Nicolas Bourbon in the post, was staunchly conservative and the curriculum at the school rapidly began to reflect his anti-reform stance.[5] It was probably as a result of this that Henry Carey was removed from Woburn and placed into the care of Sir John Russell, comptroller of the royal household. The fact that the boys were being indoctrinated in traditionalist ways was bad enough, that it was being done to Henry's own son, albeit unacknowledged, was unacceptable. What influence Mary had over her son's education, if any, is not known. It can be speculated, however, that she would not have approved of his being taught the 'retrograde' ways of the traditionalists.

Gradually life returned to normal. There is nothing to allow us to think that Mary returned to the court following the executions of her sister and brother, at least in any official capacity. This does not mean, though, that she lost all contact with that glittering, dangerous world. In 1539 William Stafford was one of the men appointed to receive Anne of Cleves when she came to England to become Henry's fourth wife.[6] At the same time, Mary's daughter, Katherine Carey, was appointed as one of the new Queen's maids. Katherine, now fifteen years old, was following in her mother's footsteps by carving out a career at court. She was joined by her aunt, Jane Parker, the widow of George Boleyn, and by her mother's young cousin, Katherine Howard. The following year Katherine Carey married Francis Knollys, one of the first of the gentlemen pensioners.

Also in 1540 Mary and William Stafford, now listed as a squire of the body, were granted livery of lands, including the manors of Southboram and Hendon in Hendon Park as well as all lands in Hever and Bransted, Kent, which had belonged to Mary's late father.[7] In October 1541 Stafford exchanged the manor of Hendon for that of Uggethorpe in Yorkshire as well as various tenements belonging to Leith in Yorkshire formerly belonging to the priory of Gisbourne.[8] Just over a year later he would be paid £82 for the overplus of Hendon and other lands in Kent sold to the King.[9] The financial situation of the Staffords was significantly eased by these acquisitions and Mary's life followed a more peaceful and settled course.

Still, fate was to disturb the smooth waters of her life one more time as King Henry's marital adventures again touched her family. The King had disliked Anne of Cleves from the moment he set eyes upon her. Immediately he sought ways toescape from his obligation to marry her, but to no avail. The marriage went ahead and Henry lived in misery until his eye fell upon a young woman in the Queen's entourage, Katherine Howard.

Katherine was the daughter of Lord Edmund Howard, who was the younger brother to Mary's uncle, Thomas Howard, third Duke of Norfolk. She was very young, probably only fifteen years of age when she entered the service of Anne of Cleves and came to the notice of Henry.[10]

The period when Katherine came into Henry's life was significant. Henry still had only one legitimate son. This was not enough to secure the dynasty; his own elder brother, Arthur, had died at the age of fifteen. Arthur, newly married, had not produced a child who would take the reins of the kingdom and so Henry had become the last hope of the Tudors. It prayed on Henry's mind that, should Edward die, there was no spare this time; the Tudor dynasty would die with Henry VIII.

Notwithstanding this, Henry had not even been able to consummate his marriage to Anne of Cleves. The failings in his sex life placed an added burden on the King, who prided himself on his masculinity. He also never forgot the humiliation of the revelation at the trial of George Boleyn, where it became known to all that Henry's sexual ability was lacking. He had to provide for his kingdom and he had to prove, if only to himself, that he was, as he implicitly asserted to Chapuys, a man like other men. Henry's insecurities were skilfully played upon by Katherine's uncle, the Duke of Norfolk, who saw her as a means of restoring his flagging fortunes. With impeccable timing, Norfolk brought his niece to the notice of the King.

With her peaches and cream complexion, her sparkling eyes of hazel and her long flowing locks of a rich dark blonde, Katherine was the very essence of English beauty. Her petite doll-like stature, her youth and vivacity, all added to her attractions and, in a short space of time, King Henry was smitten.

Mary, from the safety of her father's estate at Rochford, could only stand by as the same pattern reasserted itself. It did not vary. Henry, tired of his wife, looked for diversion. That diversion became something more substantial as Henry persuaded himself that the new woman in his life would give him sons. He dreamed about making her his wife. Then, the decision having been made, it was a simple matter of finding a way to bring the King's desire to fruition.

Henry was extremely happy with his new wife. Katherine was his 'rose without a thorn'. However, before she had come to him, Katherine already had a less than honest reputation. Her youth and inexperience were cruelly manipulated by the very people who had been appointed to take care of her. She had fallen in love, or thought she had, with Francis Dereham, a man she had met prior to her marriage to Henry. Dereham had asserted that they had pledged to marry; an assertion that could have saved both their lives had Katherine the wit to admit to it. However, another relationship, with Thomas Culpepper, had begun after her marriageto the King. This sealed her fate and Katherine went to the scaffold.

There was to be no merciful decapitation by sword for Katherine as there had been for her cousin, Anne Boleyn. Katherine was beheaded by axe, a clumsy and unwieldy weapon unless the headsman knew well how to handle it. Luckily for Katherine her head was taken off with a single stroke. Her lady in waiting and accomplice in her sexual adventures, Jane Parker, Viscountess Rochford, Mary's sister-in-law, also went to the block, her path made slippery by the blood of her mistress.

On 13 February 1542, then, Mary Boleyn lost two more of her relatives to the headsman. The demise of her cousin followed an extensive investigation into her activities. Ironically, William Stafford might have been among those who had testified against her. For, in December 1541, the name of Stafford appears among those who spoke of the Queen's relationship with Francis Dereham.[11]

No more is heard of Mary until May 1543, when she and William were granted livery of lands belonging to Mary's grandmother, Margaret Boleyn, by way of jointure.[12] Two months later, on 30 July 1543, Mary died at Rochford Hall. She was about forty-three years old. It is not known where she is buried; logic would dictate that her tomb should be at Rochford, but if she does rest there, her grave is unmarked. Just two weeks before her death Mary's formerlover, King Henry, had married his sixth wife, Katherine Parr, but he was never again to find the peace and the love he had shared with Mary.

Notes

Abbreviations:

CPR – *Calendar of the Patent Rolls preserved in the Public Record Office...
Henry VII*
CSP – *Calendar of State Papers, Domestic Series, of the reign
of Elizabeth I*
CSP Spain – *Calendar of Letters... and State Papers... between England and
Spain, 1536–1538*
CSP Venice – *Calendar of State Papers Relating to English Affairs in the
Archives of Venice*
DNB – *Oxford Dictionary of National Biography*
LP – *Letters and Papers, Foreign and Domestic, Henry VIII*

Chapter 1: The Early Years, 1500–1514
1. Emery, pp.355-357
2. Brooke, p.187
3. Brooke, p.250
4. Weever, p.514; p.799
5. Weever, p.799
6. *The Berkeley Manuscripts*
7. Collins, *Peerage*, 3.315
8. Ives, *Anne Boleyn*, p.17
9. Warnicke, *Rise and Fall*, p.34
10. *LP*, V.585
11. *CSP* Elizabeth, vol. 264, pp.510-511
12. *LP*, XI.17
13. *CPR* Henry VII, i.349
14. *CPR* Henry VII, i.357
15. Strickland, IV, p.161
16. *Anecdotes and Traditions*, p.16
17. *LP*, 1.3370
18. cited Paget, *Youth of Anne Boleyn*, p.166
19. Starkey, *Six Wives*, p.258
20. Fraser, *Six Wives*, p.120

Chapter 2: Mary in France, 1514–1520
1. *LP*, I.5483
2. *Rutland Papers*, p.25
3. *LP*, I.5484
4. *LP*, 1.5488
5. *LP*, II.1281
6. *LP*, II.411
7. *LP*, I.5495
8. Cotton MS. Caligula, D.VI. fol.249; Wood, *Letters* 1.pp.187-189
9. *LP*, II.222
10. *LP*, X.450
11. Ashdown; Bruce, p.23
12. Hughes *DNB*; Bruce, p.19
13. Ives, *Anne Boleyn*, p.35; Denny, *Anne Boleyn*, p. 38; Loades, pp.37-38
14. Bruce, p.23

Chapter 3: First Marriage, 'Lady Carey' 1520
1. IV, p.194
2. Bruce, p.23-24
3. Plowden, *Tudor Women*, p.45
4. cited in Stone, p.190
5. Stone, pp.183-184
6. *LP*, III, p.1539

Chapter 4: Golden Days, 1520–1522
1. *CSP Spain, Further suppl.* (1513–1542), pp.30-31
2. *LP* III.1994
3. *LP* III, p.ccccxxxii

Chapter 5: Kindness to a King, Mary and Henry VIII, 1522–1524
1. Hall, *Union*, p.631
2. Murphy, pp.24-25
3. Bernard, *DNB*
4. *CSP Venice*, IV, 694
5. Denny, *Anne Boleyn*, p.28
6. Ives, *Anne Boleyn*, p.16
7. *LP*, III, 2074 (5)
8. Fox, *Jane Boleyn*, p.51
9. *LP*, III, 2297 (12)
10. *LP*, III, 2994 (26)
11. *LP*, III, 3358

Chapter 6: A Turning Point, 1524
1. *LP*, V.1114
2. Cavendish, *Life of Cardinal Wolsey*, pp.121-122
3. Denny, *Anne Boleyn*, p.50
4. Hall, *Union*, p.707
5. Sander, p.32-33

6. *LP*, IV.2218 (12), 464 (18)
7. L'Estrange, vol.1, p.192
8. *LP*, IV. 2218 (12)
9. *Six Wives*, p.274

Chapter 7: King Henry VIII's Children? 1524–1526
1. *LP*, XV.901, 902
2. *LP*, VI.351
3. *LP*, XXI.712
4. Scott-Warren, *DNB*
5. *Fragmenta Regalia*, 1641, p.29
6. Edwards, *The Edwards Legacy*, p.22
7. *LP*, XIV.572
8. Varlow, *Latin Dictionary*, p.321; appendix
9. Varlow, *DNB*
10. Historical Manuscripts Commission, *Salisbury MSS*, i.400, 415, item 1314; Varlow, *DNB*
11. Varlow, *DNB*
12. *LP*, VIII.567
13. Aungier, p. 142
14. *LP*, IV.464 (15)
15. *LP*, IV.464 (18)
16. *LP*, IV.2002 (20)
17. *LP*, XV.822
18. *LP*, XV.823
19. *LP*, XVI.898
20. *LP*, XVI.1334
21. Starkey, *Six Wives*, p.670
22. Denny, *Katherine Howard*, pp120-121
23. Weir, *Henry VIII*, p.222
24. Ives, *Anne Boleyn*, p.17

Chapter 8: Out of Favour, 1526–1528
1. *LP*, IV.1939
2. Hui, Website
3. *LP*, IV.546
4. Walpole, *Catalogue*, p.64
5. *CSP Venice*, IV, p.105
6. Gairdner, 'New Lights', p. 685
7. cited in Lingard, *A Vindication*, p.106
8. Scarisbrick, p.161
9. Ives, *DNB*
10. Gairdner 'New Lights', pp.700-701
11. *Chronicle*, p.625
12. Flood, p.152
13. Flood, p.171
14. Flood, p.164
15. *LP*, IV.4409

16. *LP* IV, 4409
17. *LP*, IV.4408
18. *LP*, IV.4410
19. Warnicke, *Rise and Fall*, p.82
20. *LP*, V.11
21. *LP*, IV.4477
22. *House of Commons* 3.627
23. *LP*, V, p.306

Chapter 9: Mary Eclipsed, 1529–1532
 1. *LP*, IV.5248
 2. *Correspondance*, 1.105
 3. *LP*, IV.6085
 4. *CSP Spain 1529–1530*, p.366
 5. Nicolas, p.346

Chapter 10: The Queen's Sister, 1532–1534
 1. Hall, *Union*, p.793-794; *Tudor Tracts*, p.7; *LP*, V.1484
 2. *LP*, V.686
 3. Wyatt, *The Life of Queen Anne Boleigne*, pp.429-430
 4. *LP*, VI.923
 5. *LP*, XII.952
 6. Sander, p.27
 7. Wriothesley, 1, pp.21-22; *LP*, VI.585
 8. Ives, *Anne Boleyn*, pp.183-184
 9. *LP*, VI.1112

Chapter 11: Second Marriage, 'love overcame reason', 1534–1536
 1. Wynkyn de Worde, p.37
 2. *LP*, IV.2217
 3. *LP*, IV.5508
 4. *LP*, IV.6072
 5. *LP*, VI.562
 6. *LP* VII.177
 7. *LP* V.148
 8. Chapman, p.169
 9. *LP* VII.114
 10. *LP* VII.1013
 11. Dewhurst, *Alleged miscarriages*, p.55
 12. *LP*, VII.1193
 13. *LP*, VII.1554
 14. *LP*, VI.589
 15. Wood, vol 2, pp.193-197; *LP*, VII.1655

Chapter 12: These Bloody Days, 1536
 1. *LP*, X.144
 2. *LP*, X.199
 3. *LP*, X.294

4. *LP*, X.282
5. *LP*, X.352
6. *LP*, X.283
7. *LP*, X.450
8. *LP*, X. 351
9. British Library, Cotton MS Otho C x, fol.225
10. *LP*, X.896
11. *LP*, X.909; *CSP Spain* 1536–1538, p.121
12. Bray, pp.96-97
13. Cavendish, *Wolsey*, pp.464-465

Chapter 13: The Bitter End, 1536–1543
1. *LP*, XIV.854
2. *LP*, XIII.696
3. *LP*, XIII.717
4. *LP*, XIII.1419
5. Brigden and Wilson, 'New learning', pp.398-399
6. *LP*, XIV.572
7. *LP*, XV.611
8. *LP*, XVI.1308
9. *LP*, XVII. 258
10. Denny, *Katherine Howard*, pp.8-9
11. *LP*, XVI.1416, 1469
12. *LP*, XVIII, 623

Chapter page poems by Thomas Wyatt from various sources.

Bibliography

Arber, Edward, *Tudor Tracts, 1532–1588*, (Westminster: Constable, 1902)

Ashdown, Dulcie M., *Ladies-in-waiting* (London: Barker, *c.*1976)

Aungier, George James, *The History and Antiquities of Syon Monastery, the Parish of Isleworth, and the   Chapelry of Hounslow* (London: J.B. Nichols, 1840)

Bellay, Jean du, *Correspondance du Cardinal du Bellay* (Paris: Librairie C. Klincksieck, 1969-2008)

Bernard, G.W., 'Compton, Sir William (1482?–1528)' *Oxford Dictionary of National Biography* (Oxford University Press, Sept 2004 Online edition)

Bondoff, Stanley Thomas, *The House of Commons, 1509-1558* (London: Secker & Warburgh, 1982)

Bray, Gerald Lewis, *Documents of the English Reformation 1526-1701* (London: James Clarke & Co, 2004)

Brigden, Susan and Nigel Wilson, 'New learning and Broken Friendship' *The English Historical Review*, volume 112, No.446 (April 1997), pp.396-411

BL, Cotton MS Otho C x, fol.225

Brooke, Ralph, *A catalogue and succession of the kings, princes, dukes, marquesses, earles, and viscounts of this realme of England, since the Norman Conquest, to this present yeare, 1619 Together, vvith their armes, vviues, and children: the times of their deaths and burials, with many their memorable actions. Collected by Raphe Brooke Esquire, Yorke Herauld: discouering, and reforming many errors committed, by men of other profession, and lately published in print* ... (London: Printed by William Jaggard, and sold at his house in Barbican, 1619)

Bruce, Marie Louis, *Anne Boleyn* (London: Pan Books Ltd, 1975)

Calendar of Letters... and State Papers... between England and Spain, 1536-38

Calendar of Letters... and State Papers... between England and Spain, Further supplement (1513–1542)

Calendar of the manuscripts of the most hon. the marquis of Salisbury, 1, HMC, 9 (1883)

Calendar of the Patent Rolls preserved in the Public Record Office... Henry VII

Calendar of State Papers, Domestic Series, of the reign of Elizabeth I

Calendar of State Papers Relating to English Affairs in the Archives of Venice: Volume 4, 1527–1533 (1871), pp. 291-307

Camden, William, *Annales rerum Anglicarum, et Hibernicarum, regnante Elizabetha, ad annum salutis M.D.LXXXIX. Guilielmo Camdeno authore* (London, 1615)

Carles, Lanclot de, *Épistre contenant le procès criminel faict à l'encontre de la royne Anne Boullant d'Angleterre* (Lyon)

Cavendish, George, *The Life of Cardinal Wolsey* (London: Thomas Davison, for Harding & Lepard, 1827)

Chapman, Hester W., *Anne Boleyn* (London: Jonathan Cape, 1974)

Collins, Arthur, *Collins's Peerage of England: genealogical, biographical, and historical, greatly augmented, and continued to the present day, by Egerton Brydges* (London: Printed for F.C. and J. Rivington, 1812)

Cressy, David, *Birth, marriage, and death: ritual, religion, and the life-cycle in Tudor and Stuart England* (Oxford: Oxford University Press, 1997) pp.285-375

Cotton MS. Caligula, D.VI. fol.249

Denny, Joanna, *Anne Boleyn* (London: Portrait, 2004)

Denny, Joanna, *Katherine Howard: A Tudor Conspiracy* (London: Portrait, 2005)

Dewhurst, John, 'The Alleged Miscarriages of Catherine of Aragon and Anne Boleyn', *Medical History*, 1984, 28, pp.49-56

Dugdale, William, *Monasticon Anglicanum* (London: Bohn, 1846)

Edwards, D., *The Edwardes Legacy* (Baltimore: Gateway, 1992)

Emery, Anthony, *Greater Medieval Houses of England and Wales, 1300-1500: Southern England* (Cambridge University Press, 2006)

Flood, John L., '"Safer on the Battlefield than in the City": England, the "sweating sickness", and the continent', *Renaissance Studies* volume 17, no. 2, pp.147-176

Fox, Julia, *Jane Boleyn, The Infamous Lady Rochford* (London: Phoenix, 2007)

Fraser, Antonia, *The Six Wives of Henry VIII* (London: Weidenfeld and Nicolson, 1992)

Gairdner, James, 'New Lights on the Divorce of Henry VIII' *The English Historical Review*, volume 11, No.44 (Oct 1896), pp.673-702

Hall, Edward *The Union of the Two Noble and Illustre Families of York and Lancaster*, ed H. Ellis (London: Printed for J. Johnson..., 1809)

Holinshed, Raphael, *Chronicle of England, Scotland and Ireland*, ed. John Hooker (London, 1586)

Hughes, Jonathan, 'Stafford, Mary (c.1499–1543)', *Oxford Dictionary of National Biography* (Oxford University Press, Sept 2004 Online edition)

Hui, Roland, *A Reassessment of Queen Anne Boleyn's Portraiture*: http://www.geocities.com/rolandhui_2000/ab_portraiture.htm

Ives, Eric, *The Life and Death of Anne Boleyn: 'the most happy'* (Oxford: Blackwell Publishing Ltd, 2004)

Ives, Eric, 'Anne (c.1500–1536)' *Oxford Dictionary of National Biography* (Oxford University Press, Sept 2004 Online edition)

Jerdan, William, *Rutland papers. Original documents illustrative of the courts and times of Henry VII and Henry VIII. Selected from the private archives of His Grace the Duke of Rutland by William Jerdan* (London: Camden Society, [OS 21] 1842)

L'Estrange, Alfred Guy Kingham, *The palace and the hospital; or, chronicles of Greenwich* two volumes (London: Hurst & Blackett, 1886)

Letters and Papers, Foreign and Domestic, Henry VIII

Lingard, *A Vindication of certain passages in the fourth and fifth volumes of the History of England* (London: Printed for J. Mawman, 1826)

Loades, D.M., *The Politics of Marriage: Henry VIII and his Queens* (Stroud: Alan Sutton, 1994)

Murphy, Beverley A., *Bastard Prince: Henry VIII's Lost Son* (Stroud, Sutton Publishing, 2001)

Naunton, Robert, *Fragmenta Regalia* (Westminster: Constable, 1895)

Nichols, John Gough (ed.), *The Herald and Genealogist*, volume 4

Nicolas, Nicholas Harris, *The privy purse expences of King Henry the Eighth: from November 1529 to December 1532...* (London: Pickering, 1827)

Oxford Dictionary of National Biography online edition

Paget, H., 'The youth of Anne Boleyn', *Bulletin of the Institute of Historical Research*, 54 (1981), 162-70

Peters, Christine, 'Gender, Sacrament and Ritual: The Making and Meaning of Marriage in Late Medieval and Early Modern England', *Past and Present*, 169, pp.63-96

Plowden, Alison, *Tudor Women*: Queens and Commoners (London: Weidenfeld and Nicolson, 1979)

Revised Standard Version

Sander, Nicholas, *De Origine at Progressu Schismatzs Anglicani* (Rome: 1585)

Sarum Missal

Scarrisbrick, J.J., *Henry VIII* (London: Methuen, 1990)

Scott-Warren, Jason, 'Harington, John (c.1517–1582), *Oxford Dictionary of National Biography* (Oxford University Press, Sept 2004 Online edition)

Smyth of Nibley, John, *The Berkeley Manuscripts*, ed. Sir John MacLean (Gloucester: John Bellows, 1883–1885)

Starkey, David, *Six Wives: The Queens of Henry VIII* (London: Vintage, 2004)

Stone, L., 'Marriage among the English Nobility in the 16th and 17th Centuries' *Comparative Studies in Society and History*, pp. 182-260

Strickland, Agnes, *Lives of the queens of England, from the Norman conquest; with anecdotes of their courts, now first published from official records and other authentic documents, private as well as public* (London: Henry Colburn, 1840–1849)

Thoms, William J., *Anecdotes and Traditions* (London: Camden Society, OS 5, 1839)

Varlow, Sally, 'Sir Francis Knollys's Latin dictionary: new evidence for Katherine Carey', *Historical Research*, volume 80, no. 209 (August 2007)

Varlow, Sally, 'Knollys, Katherine, Lady Knollys (c.1523–1569), *Oxford Dictionary of National Biography* (Oxford University Press, Sept 2004 Online edition)

Walpole, Horace, *A Catalogue of the Royal and Noble Authors of England, with Lists of their Works* (Edinburgh: printed for W. H. Lunn, Cambridge; J. Mundell & Co. Edinburgh; and for J. Mundell, College, Glasgow, 1796)

Warnicke, Retha M., *The Rise and Fall of Anne Boleyn: Family Politics at the Court of Henry VIII* (New York: Cambridge University Press, 1989)

Weever, John, *Ancient funerall monuments within the vnited monarchie of Great Britaine, Ireland, and the islands adiacent with the dissolued monasteries therein contained: their founders, and what eminent persons haue beene in the same interred. As also the death and buriall of certaine of the bloud royall; the nobilitie and gentrie of these kingdomes entombed in forraine nations. A worke reuiuing the dead memory of the royall progenie, the nobilitie, gentrie, and communaltie, of these his Maiesties dominions. Intermixed and illustrated with variety of historicall obseruations, annotations, and briefe notes, extracted out of approued authors ... Whereunto is prefixed a discourse of funerall monuments ... Composed by the studie and trauels of Iohn Weeuer* (London : Printed by Thomas Harper. 1631. And are to be sold by Laurence Sadler at the signe of the Golden Lion in little Britaine, 1631)

Weir, Alison, *Henry VIII: King & Court* (London: Pimlico, 2002)

Wood, Mary Anne Everett, *Letters of Royal and Illustrious Ladies of Great Britain* (London: Henry Colburn, 1846), 2 volumes

Wriothesley, Charles, *A Chronicle of England During the Reigns of the Tudors, from A.D. 1585 to 1559* (London: Camden Society, New Series, 11, 1875)

Wyatt, Thomas, *The Poetical Works of Sir Thomas Wyatt* (London: William Pickering, 1831)

Wynkyn de Worde, *The Babees Book*, Early English Texts Society OS 32

Acknowledgements

Biographers often do not choose their subjects, their subjects choose them. When I was invited to write a biography of a Tudor woman, the one who suggested herself to me was Mary Boleyn. Perhaps the most attractive thing about Mary was the fact that she is very easy to overlook. The sister of the woman who was, perhaps, Henry VIII's most engaging Queen, Mary is often a mere footnote to Anne's story. In fact, Mary has fared better in the world of romance than history. She captured the imagination of novelists, who have taken her story and used it as a springboard to explore the Tudor court, with its glamour, intrigue and courtly love. She is, then, perhaps better known as a fictional character than a historical figure. Scholarship has largely ignored the real Mary Boleyn, at least until now. This biography seeks to redress the situation, presenting Mary for the first time as a subject, as a person, in her own right.

Every author has people to thank for the help they received during the writing process. My thanks go to Anna L. Spender at Hever Castle, who supplied photographs of Mary and Hever. Our chat about Mary and Anne was both interesting and inspiring. I also wish to thank Henry A. Fitzhugh for the photograph of William Carey and the interesting and encouraging comments he made about my work. Thanks also go to Anne Isba for being kind enough to proof read this work – any errors are, however, my own. Lastly I would like to thank Jonathan Reeve for showing me that writing about women's lives could be every bit as interesting and challenging as writing about men.

List of Illustrations

Index

Index

Hoo, Ann 14
Hopkins, Nicholas 70
Hornebolt, Lucas 100–1
Howard, Elizabeth, Countess of Wiltshire and
  Ormond 15, 16, 19, 39, 54, 134–5, 172
Howard family 15–16
Howard, John, Duke of Norfolk 15–16
Howard, Katherine, Queen of England 81, 92,
  93, 175–7
Howard, Thomas, Earl of Surrey, Duke of
  Norfolk (elder) 15–16
Howard, Thomas, Earl of Surrey, Duke of
  Norfolk (younger) 54, 158, 176
Hunt, Thomas 143

Jordan, Isabelle 116

Katherine of Aragon, Queen of England 17–18,
  24, 49, 61
  annulment of marriage to Henry 103–7,
    123, 126, 133, 166
  death of 155–7
  discarded by Henry 71–3, 94
  early life 69–70
  and Mary Boleyn 76
  pregnancies 71, 80
  resists annulment 120
  support for 108–11
Katherine of Lancaster 69–70
Kingston, William 142, 143
Knollys, Francis 19, 87, 88, 174

L'Estrange, Alfred Guy Kingham 77
Lives of the Berkeleys (Smyth) 10
Louis XII, King of France 24, 27–30

Malte, John 85
Margaret of Austria 19–21, 25–6
Margaret of York 20
Mary, Princess, later Mary I 71, 72, 103, 161,
  166, 168
Maximilian, Emperor 24
More, Thomas 14
Mortimer, Margaret 34, 104

Naunton, Robert 86
Neuenahr, Hermann von 112
Norris, Henry 162, 163, 165

Page, Richard 163, 164
Parker, Arabella 62
Parker, Henry, Lord Morley 102
Parker, Jane 57, 101–2, 174, 177
Parker, Margery 62
Parr, Katherine, Queen of England 81, 177
Pasqualigo, Pietro 31–2
Percy, Henry later Earl of Northumberland 74,
  110, 167
Penshurst Place 67
Perrot, John 86
Plantagenet, Arthur, Viscount Lisle 143
Plantagenet, Honor, Viscountess Lisle 143–4
Pole, Henry, Lord Montague 109
Pole, Margaret, Countess of Salisbury 108–9
Pole, Reginald 105–6
Popincourt, Jane 61, 92

Poynings, Edward 18
Prestwich, James 173

Richard III 14, 15–16, 85

Sander, Nicholas 76
Seymour, Jane, Queen of England 81, 101, 160,
  168, 171
Skip, John 160–1
Smeaton, Mark 163
Smyth, John, of Nibley 10
Spencer, Margaret 42
Spencer, Robert 42
Stafford, Edward, Duke of Buckingham 60, 67,
  70–1, 109, 141, 143
Stafford, William (Mary's second husband)
  banished from court 148–54
  at court 174, 177
  grants and awards 174
  marriage to Mary Boleyn 140–4, 171
  religious sympathies 145
  social position 146, 152–3
Starkey, David 78
Stucley, Thomas 85–6
Suffolk, Duchess of see Tudor, Mary, Queen of
  France, Duchess of Suffolk
Suffolk, Duke of see Brandon, Charles, Duke
  of Suffolk
  sweating sickness 111–13
Symonds, William 67

Thoms, William J. 19
Throckmorton, George 135
Tudor, Mary, Queen of France, Duchess of
  Suffolk 23–30, 57, 128
Tyndale, William 124–5

Volg, Johann 112

Walpole, Horace 102
Weever, John 10
Weston, Francis 163–4
Wier, Johann 112
Wolsey, Thomas 34–5, 39, 46, 49, 105, 113,
  120
  downfall 120–2
  at the Field of Cloth of Gold 50–2
Wyatt, Henry 18
Wyatt, Thomas 18, 73, 163, 164

Young, John 18

191

Tudor History from Amberley Publishing

THE TUDORS
Richard Rex

'The best introduction to England's most important dynasty'
DAVID STARKEY
'Gripping and told with enviable narrative skill... a delight'
THES
'Vivid, entertaining and carrying its learning lightly'
EAMON DUFFY
'A lively overview' **THE GUARDIAN**

£20.00   978-1-84868-049-4   272 pages HB 143 illus., 64 col

MARGARET OF YORK
Christine Weightman

'A pioneering biography of the Tudor dynasty's most
dangerous enemy'
PROFESSOR MICHAEL HICKS
'Christine Weightman brings Margaret alive once more'
THE YORKSHIRE POST
'A fascinating account of a remarkable woman'
THE BIRMINGHAM POST

£14.99   978-1-84868-099-9   208 pages PB 40 illus

CATHERINE HOWARD
Lacey Baldwin Smith

'A brilliant, compelling account' **ALISON WEIR**
'A faultless book' **THE SPECTATOR**
'Lacey Baldwin Smith has so excellently caught the
atmosphere of the Tudor age' **THE OBSERVER**

£9.99   978-1-84868-521-5   256 pages PB 25 col illus

THE SIX WIVES OF HENRY VIII
David Loades

'Neither Starkey nor Weir has the assurance and command
of Loades' **SIMON HEFFER, LITERARY REVIEW**
'Incisive and profound. I warmly recommend this book'
ALISON WEIR

£9.99   978-1-4456-0049-9   256 pages PB 55 illus, 31 col

ANNE BOLEYN
Elizabeth Norton

£9.99 978-1-84868-514-7
224 pages PB 55 illus, 36 col

MARY BOLEYN
Josephine Wilkinson

£9.99 978-1-84868-525-3
208 pages PB 22 illus, 10 col

JANE SEYMOUR
Elizabeth Norton

£9.99 978-1-84868-527-7
224 pages PB 53 illus, 26 col

HENRY VIII
Richard Rex

£9.99 978-1-84868-098-2
192 pages PB 81 illus, 48 col

ELIZABETH I
Richard Rex

£9.99 978-1-84868-423-
192 pages PB 75 illus

THE EARLY LOVES OF ANNE BOLEYN
Josephine Wilkinson
£20.00 978-1-84868-430-0
224 pages HB 34 illus, 17 col

CATHERINE PARR
Elizabeth Norton
£18.99 978-1-84868-582-6
320 pages HB 52 illus, 39 col

ANNE OF CLEVES
Elizabeth Norton
£20.00 978-1-84868-329-7
224 pages HB 54 illus, 27 col

ANNE BOLEYN
P. Friedmann
£20.00 978-1-84868-827-8
352 pages HB 47 illus, 20 col

Available from all good bookshops or to order direct
Please call **01285-760-030 www.amberleybooks.com**